All of local society is abuzz with rumors that the wedding of the year—between the heiress of a certain *very* old Eastwick family and her *almost* equally well-connected fiancé—might not happen.

Of course, *this* wedding has been postponed so many times that some people wondered whether the bride was really ready to get married. But we thought she meant it this time. The wedding invitations have been chosen, and all the arrangements—right down to the name cards and the place settings—have been made.

And yet we hear the bride-to-be is having second thoughts. Hmm... Could that have *anything* to do with the sudden reappearance in our little town of another man— a very handsome, very troublesome man the lady is rumored to have been, um... "involved" with years ago...?

Dear Reader,

Things are heating up in our family dynasty series, THE ELLIOTTS, with *Heiress Beware* by Charlene Sands. Seems the rich girl has gotten herself into a load of trouble and has ended up in the arms of a sexy Montana stranger. (Well...there are worse things that could happen.)

We've got miniseries galore this month, as well. There's the third book in Maureen Child's wonderful SUMMER OF SECRETS series, *Satisfying Lonergan's Honor,* in which the hero learns a startling fifteen-year-old secret. And our high-society continuity series, SECRET LIVES OF SOCIETY WIVES, features *The Soon-To-Be-Disinherited Wife* by Jennifer Greene. Also, Emilie Rose launches a brand-new trilogy about three socialites who use their trust funds to purchase bachelors at a charity auction. TRUST FUND AFFAIRS gets kicked off right with *Paying the Playboy's Price.*

June also brings us the second title in our RICH AND RECLUSIVE series, which focuses on wealthy, mysterious men. *Forced to the Altar,* Susan Crosby's tale of a woman at the mercy of a...yes...wealthy, mysterious man, will leave you breathless. And rounding out the month is Cindy Gerard's emotional tale of a pregnant heroine who finds a knight in shining armor with *A Convenient Proposition.*

So start your summer off right with all the delectable reads from Silhouette Desire.

Happy reading!

Melissa Jeglinski

Melissa Jeglinski
Senior Editor
Silhouette Books

Please address questions and book requests to:
Silhouette Reader Service
U.S.: 3010 Walden Ave., P.O. Box 1325, Buffalo, NY 14269
Canadian: P.O. Box 609, Fort Erie, Ont. L2A 5X3

JENNIFER GREENE

The Soon-To-Be-Disinherited Wife

Silhouette®

Desire

Published by Silhouette Books
America's Publisher of Contemporary Romance

Acknowledgment
Special thanks and acknowledgment is given to Jennifer Greene for her contribution to the Secret Lives of Society Wives miniseries.

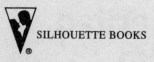 SILHOUETTE BOOKS

ISBN 0-373-76731-5

THE SOON-TO-BE-DISINHERITED WIFE

Visit Silhouette Books at www.eHarlequin.com

Printed in U.S.A.

JENNIFER GREENE

lives near Lake Michigan with her husband and two children. Before writing full-time, she worked as a teacher and a personnel manager. Michigan State University honored her as an "outstanding woman graduate" for her work with women on campus.

Ms. Greene has written more than fifty category romances, for which she has won numerous awards, including two RITA® Awards from the Romance Writers of America in the Best Short Contemporary Books category, and a Career Achievement Award from *Romantic Times BOOKclub.*

One

Emma Dearborn felt an itch. Not a little itch. A maddening, unrelenting itch—right between her shoulder blades, where she couldn't reach it.

Emma wasn't prone to itches and was almost never guilty of fidgeting, which was probably why she remembered experiencing the same terrorizing itch sensation before. It had only happened twice in her life. The first time, she'd accidentally driven her dad's restored priceless Morgan into Long Island Sound at Greenwich Point when she was sixteen. The car had been recovered; her dad nearly hadn't. The other time, her date for the annual Christmas cotillion had turned ugly, and she'd had to walk home in her long white satin dress and heels in a snowstorm, crying the whole time.

Since those days, of course, she was no longer a novice with driving or men. More to the point, the itch this time couldn't possibly relate to some impending traumatic event. Her life was going splendiferously.

Impatiently she took a long gulp of mint-raspberry tea. Mentally she told herself to get over the damned itch and quit squirming. For Pete's sake, there was nothing remotely wrong. Everything around her reflected her serenely contented life.

"Emma?"

A basking-warm June sun soaked through the glass windows overlooking the pool outside. The Emerald Room was the one place in the Eastwick Country Club where members could dress casually. Today the pool was chock-full of kids fresh out of school and shrieking with joyful energy. Inside, moms in sandals and shorts elbowed with the business-lunch crowd in suits.

Emma, because she'd just chaired a meeting of the fund-raising committee, was stuck dressed on the formal side. Her light silk sheath was lavender-blue, not because it was her signature color. Emma objected to the whole pretentious concept of signature colors. Somehow, though, her closet mysteriously filled up with blues. Everyone else in the group was dressed more laid-back—not that anyone cared today about clothes.

The Debs had missed their traditional lunch last month—everyone was so darn busy!—which meant they all had to talk at once to catch up.

Harry, the bartender, had kindly reserved the malachite table by the doors, not just giving them the best view but also a little privacy for their gossip. Felicity and Vanessa and Abby were all there.

Emma's heart warmed to the laughter—even if that itch

was still driving her crazy. The friends were closer than sisters. They'd all grown up together, attended the same private school, knew each other's most embarrassing moments—and tended to bring them out at these lunches. If the teasing ever lagged, there was always their debutante history to haul out of storage. What were friends for if not to savor and embellish the most mortifying events in one's life? And Caroline Keating-Spence had joined them for lunch this time.

"Emma, are you sleeping?"

Quickly she whipped her head toward Felicity, not realizing that she'd dropped out of the conversation. "Not sleeping, honest. Just kind of woolgathering what a long history we have together…how much fun we've always had."

"Yeah, sure." Vanessa winked to the rest of them. "She covered up nicely, but we all know she's engaged. Naturally she wasn't listening to us. She's at that moony stage."

Felicity chuckled. "Either that or that big clunk of a sapphire on her finger is blinding her. Hells bells, it blinds the rest of us, too. What an original engagement ring. But that's exactly what I was trying to ask you about, Em. How's everything going with the wedding plans?"

Again she felt that exasperating itch spider up her spine. This was getting downright crazy. Her engagement to Reed Kelly was yet another thing that was going totally—*totally*—right in her life. At twenty-nine years old, she'd stopped believing she'd ever be married.

Actually the truth was that she'd never wanted to be.

"Everything's going fine," she assured them all, "except that Reed seems to have arranged the whole honeymoon before we've finalized the wedding plans."

They all laughed. "You two *have* set a date, though, right?"

Another shooting itch. "Actually we've reserved Eastwick's ballroom for two different Saturdays, but between my schedule at the gallery and Reed's racing schedule with the horses, we still haven't pinned one down for sure. I promise, this group will be the first to know. In fact, you'll probably know before I do, knowing how fast this group picks up secrets."

They all chortled—and agreed—and then moved on to the next victim. Felicity, being Eastwick's foremost wedding planner—which meant that she excelled in both original extravaganzas and gossip—was always full of news.

As the freshest scandals were brought out to air, Emma glanced at Caroline, who seemed oddly quiet. Of course, it was hard to get a word in with the Debs all talking simultaneously, but Caroline hadn't joined in the laughter. And now Emma noticed her signaling Harry for her third glass of wine.

The itch was close to driving Emma to drink, too, but seeing Caroline guzzling down pinot noir distracted her. Heaven knew, the Debs had been known to enjoy a drink— and occasionally to overindulge. No one kiss and told in the group, not on each other. Emma wouldn't normally care if Caroline was gulping down the pinot noirs, but drinking was so unlike her.

Caroline wasn't one of the original core Debs group because she was a little younger. Emma had swooped her into the circle of friends, the same way she tended to peel wallflowers off the wall at social gatherings. Caroline was no wallflower, but there was a time she'd needed a little boost of self-confidence. Emma had gotten to know her well because of Garrett—Caroline's older brother.

Again Emma felt a ticklish itch. This time a familiar one. Although her heart hadn't dug up that old emotional history in a blue moon, Garrett Keating had been her first love. Just picturing him brought back that whole poignant era—the time in her life when she'd still believed in love, when she'd felt crazy-high just to be in the same room with him and equally pit-low miserable every second they'd had to be apart.

Everybody had to lose that silly idealism sometime, she knew. Still, she'd always regretted their breaking up before making love. Back then she'd held on to her virginity like a gambler unwilling to lay down her aces, yet so often since then she thought she'd missed the right time with the right man. Garrett's kisses had awakened her sexuality, her first feelings of power as a woman…her first feelings of vulnerability and surrender, as well. She'd never forgotten him, never even tried. She wasn't carrying a torch or anything foolish like that; it was just a first-love thing. He owned a corner of her heart, always would…. Abruptly Emma stopped woolgathering. Harry showed up at their table again.

The bartender served Caroline her third wine, which she immediately downed like water. Emma frowned. Everyone knew Caroline had had a rift with her husband, Griff, the year before—but they were back together now. Everyone had seen them nuzzling each other at the spring art fair as if they were new lovers. So what was the heavy deal with the wine?

"*Murder!*" someone said.

Emma's head shot up. "Say what?"

Abby spoke up from the corner, her voice a thousand

times more tentative than normal. "You've had your head in the clouds, Em. I don't blame you, with a wedding coming up. But I was just telling the group what happened since I went to the police about my mother."

"The police?" Emma knew about Abby's mother's death. Everyone did. Lucinda Baldwin—alias Bunny—had created the *Eastwick Social Diary*, which had dished all the dirt on the moneyed crowd in Eastwick. Marriages, cheating, divorces, touchy habits, legal or business indiscretions—if it was scandal worthy, Bunny somehow always knew and loved to tell. Her death had been a shock to everyone. "I know how young your mom was, Abby. But I thought someone said she had a heart condition that hadn't been detected before, that that was what she died from—"

"That's what I thought originally, too," Abby affirmed. "But right after Mom died, I couldn't face going through her things. It took me a while…but when I finally got around to opening my mom's private safe, I just expected to find her journals and jewelry. The jewelry was there, but all her journals were gone. Stolen. They had to be. It was the only place she ever kept them. That's when I first started worrying. And then, finding out that someone tried to blackmail Jack Cartright because of information in those missing journals added to my suspicions."

"Abby's become more and more concerned that her mom was murdered," Felicity clarified.

"My God." Scandal was one thing, but Eastwick barely needed an active police force. There hadn't been a serious crime in the community in years, much less anything as grave as murder.

"I can't sleep at night," Abby admitted. "I just can't stop

thinking about it. My mom loved secrets. Loved putting together the *Diary*. And for darn sure, she loved scandals. But she never had a mean bone in her body. She had tons of things written down in her journals that she never used in the *Diary* because she didn't want to hurt people."

Emma groped to understand. "So that's partly why you think she was murdered? Because someone stole those journals? Either because they wanted to use the information, or because they had a secret themselves they wanted covered up?"

"Exactly. But I still can't prove it," Abby said restlessly. "I mean, the journals are gone. That's for sure. But I can't prove the theft is related to her death. The police keep telling me that I don't have enough to open up a new inquest. Honestly, they've been really nice—they all agree the situation sounds suspicious. But there's no one to arrest, no suspects. I can't even prove the journals were stolen."

"But she's positive they were," Felicity filled in.

Abby nodded. "They *had* to be stolen. The safe is the only place my mother ever kept them. Unfortunately, the police can't act just because I know something is true. There's no evidence to prove my mother didn't simply hide the journals somewhere else. And there isn't a single suspect."

The whole group clustered close to discuss the disturbing situation—and to support Abby—but eventually the Emerald Room filled up with kids and families. Serious talk became impossible. The women lightened up, chitchatted about family news, but eventually the group broke up.

In the parking lot Emma climbed into her white SUV, her mind spinning between Caroline's troubling behavior at lunch and the worrisome suspicions about Bunny's death. Still, by the time she turned on Main Street, her mood instinctively lifted.

Her art gallery, Color, was only a couple blocks off the main drag in town. Emma didn't mind running the fundraising committee for Eastwick's country club or any of the other social responsibilities her parents pushed on her. If it weren't for her parents—and a mighty huge trust fund coming to her on her thirtieth birthday—she couldn't do the things she really loved. Most people never knew about the volunteer work she did with kids, but the whole community was well aware how much time and love she devoted to the gallery.

She parked in the narrow, crooked drive. The building was at the corner of Maple and Oak, and in June now, a profuse row of peonies bloomed inside the white picket fence. Typical of old Connecticut towns, Eastwick had tons of pre-Revolutionary history. Her building had once been a house. It was two hundred–plus years old, brick, with tall, skinny windows and a dozen small rooms— which was the advantage. Although something always seemed to need maintenance, from the plumbing to the electricity, she had a dozen rooms to display completely different kinds of artwork. Customers could roam around and examine whatever they liked in relative privacy.

By the time she bolted out of the SUV—and nearly tripped on the cobblestone steps—she was humming. A shipment of Alson Skinner Clark prints was due in late that afternoon. They needed sorting and hanging. And two weeks before, she'd come across an old Walter Farndon oil on canvas that was still stashed in the back room—her workshop—that needed cleaning and repair, which she loved doing. And a room on the second floor was vacant right now, just waiting for her to set up a display of local artists' work, another project she couldn't wait to take on.

Her gallery rode the edge of making a profit and not. Emma knew perfectly well she could have run it more efficiently, but she'd always known she had the trust fund coming. It wasn't the money that mattered to her but the freedom to open up art to the community, to be part of making something beautiful in people's lives.

She'd never told anyone how important that goal of beauty was to her. The Debs would just roll their eyes at her goofy idealism. Her family would sigh as if she'd never understand practical reality—at least, reality on their terms. And maybe all of them were right, but when Emma opened the ornate red-lacquer door into Color, she felt a sweeping burst of plain old happiness.

"Hey, Ms. Dearborn! I was hoping you'd be back by midafternoon. You got that crate from New York you were waiting for. Came in FedEx before noon." Josh, who'd worked part time for her for years, blessed her with a shy smile. He was somewhere in the vicinity of sixty, skinny as a rail and paler than paint. Some said he'd been an artist once. Some said he was gay. Some said he'd had a too-long relationship with bordeaux. All Emma knew was that he'd walked in and started helping her when she first opened the place. He'd taught her tons.

"I can't wait to get into it. You can watch for customers up front?"

"Sure thing."

She glanced at her office, stashed her summer bag and spun around to zoom in the back room when the phone rang. When she grabbed it, she heard the familiar voice of her fiancé.

"Hey, sweetheart. I was wondering if you had time for dinner tonight. I'm tied up most of the afternoon but pretty sure I could make it into town around, say, seven."

Instinctively she twisted her arm behind her to claw at that strange, aggravating itch again. The restless, stressy feeling that had been bugging her for hours suddenly fiercely intensified. "Sure," she said. "How's your day?"

"Couldn't be better. Bought a honey of a stallion…"

Standing with the phone to her ear, close to the window, she ignored the itch and suddenly, slowly lifted her hand. The sapphire on her left hand was from Sri Lanka. Reed had taken her to a jeweler, shown her a bed of sapphires, only argued when she'd first tried to pick a smaller stone. The ring was more than a breathtaking gem. It was a symbol of something she'd been so positive she'd never have.

She'd always been positive that marriage wasn't for her. She liked men fine and totally adored kids. But so many couples in Eastwick, including her parents, seemed more like business mergers than love affairs. Sex was a commodity pretty much like any other. Emma didn't knock anyone else's choices, she just never wanted that kind of life. Yet when Reed asked her to marry him, well…maybe he'd never made her heart race or her mood go giddy, but damn. He was such a good guy. Impossible not to love. When it came down to it, she'd easily said yes, recognizing that he was probably the only man she could imagine being married to.

Today, she felt no differently than she'd felt the day he'd slid the engagement ring on her finger.

It was just…she couldn't seem to quell the strange, edgy sensation of panic that had been hounding her mood for hours now. "I can't wait for tonight!" she assured him brightly.

But when she hung up the phone, guilt smacked her in the heart. What kind of goofy woman was she that she'd rather spend the evening unpacking old crates in the back of her gallery than go out to a romantic dinner with a man she loved?

Four-thirty in the afternoon, any weekday afternoon, always turned into a work frenzy. Garrett Keating had hired a driver about four years ago, not because he didn't enjoy driving himself—even in the craziness of downtown Manhattan—but because the crises automatically seemed to kick in during that late-afternoon time frame. This afternoon, typically, he'd left his investment-banking firm less than ten minutes ago, yet his cell had rung nonstop. As he sat in the backseat, his briefcase was open and papers were scattered everywhere.

"Keating," he barked into the receiver for the latest interruption.

An unfamiliar female voice answered. "Mr. Garrett Keating? Caroline Keating-Spence's brother?"

Immediate worry clawed his pulse. "Yes. What's this about?"

"Your sister asked us to call you. This is Mrs. Henry, the senior day nurse in ICU at Eastwick—"

"Oh my God. Is she all right?"

"We believe she will be, in time. But the circumstances are a little touchy. Your parents have been here, but they seem to upset your sister more than help. Because Mrs.

Keating-Spence is in such a fragile state of mind, when she asked for you—"

"I'll be there as fast as I can make arrangements. Which will be immediately. But what exactly is wrong?"

"I wouldn't normally say over the phone if your sister hadn't asked me to convey at least part of the situation. Her husband is out of the country. Her parents are possibly too upset to make the situation easier. So—"

"Just tell me."

"She took in an extensive quantity of mixed alcohol and medication." A short silence. "Her parents—your parents—are quite determined that your sister did this accidentally. No one on the medical staff has any doubt that your sister had to know exactly what she was doing." Another short silence. "I believe it best to be blunt. When she first came in, no one was sure we could bring her back. That medical crisis is over now, but—"

"I'll be there," Garrett said swiftly and disconnected.

Ed, his driver, met his eyes in the rearview mirror. "Sounds like there's a problem?"

"Yes. I have to leave town. Immediately. I'll give you a list of things I'd appreciate your handling at the apartment...."

Garrett ran nonstop for the next few hours, fear and guilt shadowing his heart. He handled millions of dollars every day, juggled a pressure-cooker workload, so how had he failed so badly at finding a few minutes for his sister?

On the long, silent drive to Eastwick, he couldn't stop thinking about Caro. He adored his sister. They'd always been thick as thieves, allied against parents who'd never had time or interest in raising children. When Caroline married, naturally Garrett had retreated. But a year ago, when he heard she was having trouble with Griff, he'd stepped back in, prepared to shoot the son of a bitch—*any* son of a bitch—who dared to hurt his sister.

All his life, though, he'd been better at work than relationships.

Business had been good, except that he'd always had a hard time putting a lid on his workaholic tendencies. Make one million, naturally he wanted to make five, then ten. He was generally connected to a computer or a phone twenty hours out of twenty-four. So maybe he had no love life or personal life, but he was thriving.

He was sure he'd been thriving.

But then Caroline had called four days ago and he just hadn't found the time to call her back. She'd called again yesterday morning. He'd been planning to call her tonight. Really. For sure.

Only, damn it, maybe he'd have forgotten that the way he forgot everything else lately. Business had consumed him tighter than a tornado wind.

His sister, who'd always counted on him—who *knew* she could count on him, who'd never doubted he'd be there for her—had needed help. And he'd flunked the course.

By the time he reached the outskirts of Eastwick, night had fallen, his stomach was churning and his heart feeling sharp-sick. It wasn't just guilt; it was caring. So many people believed he was cold-blooded—and maybe he was; that was what made him good in business. But he wasn't cold about his sister. He fiercely loved her.

He'd just failed her this time. And he couldn't, wouldn't, forgive himself.

At the hospital he locked the car and jogged for the door,

still wearing the navy suit he'd worn all day, not having eaten in God knows how long. He didn't care. He shot through the doors, jabbed the elevator button for three, ran.

He hadn't been home—much less near Eastwick General Hospital—in a blue moon and then some. But the structure hadn't noticeably changed since he was a kid. He'd have known his way around even if his family hadn't donated a wing or two over the years. Critical care was the isolated unit off the third floor in the back—the location chosen because it had a helipad on the roof.

The CC wing was quiet. The sound of machines and monitors made more noise than the patients. Lights dimmed after nine. He didn't immediately see a nurse or doctor, so simply hiked past each glass-doored cubicle, looking for his sister. The unit held only ten beds, usually more than needed even in emergency circumstances. Six beds were filled—not one of them with his sister.

Finally he found a doctor emerging from the last door. "I'm Garrett Keating. I was told my sister, Caroline Keating-Spence—"

"Yes, Mr. Keating. She was here until late this afternoon. We just moved her a couple hours ago to a private room."

"So she's better." For that instant, it was all he wanted to hear.

"You'll need to speak with her doctor, but the nurse will tell you her room—"

More rigmarole. More running. He took the stairs rather than waiting for the elevator—he'd never been good at waiting, and there wasn't a chance he could pretend to be patient tonight. Room 201. That's where they told him to go. A private room with a twenty-four-hour monitor.

Garrett suspected the monitor meant that either his sister wasn't out of the woods yet or that they feared she'd try suicide again.

Even the nurse hadn't specifically used the word *suicide,* but Garrett immediately knew what she hadn't said—because he knew his sister. This last year, once she'd mended the breach with her husband, Caroline had seemed solid and happy, not as fragile as she'd been for so long. Yet Garrett knew her. How the baggage of their childhood had affected her. How deeply she felt things. How fiercely she hid those feelings.

Some people would never buy the farm, but Caroline was always someone who couldn't quite close the gate to depression.

He scraped a hand through his hair and suddenly halted outside 201. He felt as if he'd been running hell-bent for leather for hours, which was fine but not how he wanted his sister to see him. He forced himself to stand still for a few minutes, pull it all together, concentrate on pulling off an image of calm strength.

A nurse buzzed past him. Then two aides. He took a step toward the door, when suddenly a woman walked out of Caroline's room. She almost ran straight into him—would have if he hadn't instinctively reached out to steady her.

Her head shot up. A mane of silky dark hair fell to shoulder length, framing a cameo face—elegant bones, huge eyes bluer than violet, a pale mouth with the lipstick worn off.

Her striking looks would have ransomed his attention even if he didn't know her…but he did.

Her name didn't pop into his head in that second, probably because, hell, his mind was gone after these past stress-packed hours. Yet stress or no stress, he immediately remembered her eyes. He remembered kissing her. He remembered dancing in the grass at midnight, remembered laughing...the way he never seemed to laugh with other people, not then or now. But she was different. She'd made him laugh. Made him fall harder in love than a crash.

Of course, that was aeons ago.

A lifetime and more.

"Garrett," she said gently. "I'm so glad you're here."

"Emma." He'd known her name all along. It was just that the memories had rushed into his head faster than the prosaic facts. "You've been with my sister?"

"Yes. It's past visiting hours, but..." She hesitated. "I think no one wants to leave her alone. Your parents were here until about a half hour ago. In fact, I just stayed in the hall—but I heard her talking, realized she was upset. So when I saw them leave, I went in. I didn't know what else to do. Except try to be there for her. She's fallen asleep now." Again she hesitated. A wisp of a smile softened her face. "It's good to see you."

"Not under these circumstances."

"No. In fact, I remember your saying you'd never come back to Eastwick if you could help it."

He remembered that suddenly, all too well. It was why he'd broken it off with her all those years ago—because he'd rather give up anything, everything, than live in this damn town. But that was how he'd felt at twenty-one, an age when everything was an ultimatum. An age when you assumed you didn't need anyone ever. An age when it was so amazingly easy to be self-righteous.

Now he looked at Emma and thought she'd grown into

her looks. She used to be lovely, but she'd gone far beyond lovely now. She was wearing blue pants, a dark cotton sweater. Dressed comfortably for a hospital visit, nothing fancy, but her choice of clothes showed off her long, lean body. There was pride in her posture, in her eyes. A poise she'd never had as a girl.

A loneliness.

She looked as if she wanted to say something else, but then shook her head. "You'll want to go in to see her. And I'm just leaving—"

"Emma, if you wouldn't mind…"

She cocked her head.

"I do want to see her. Right now. But if she's fallen asleep, could you wait just a couple minutes? I'd appreciate hearing your impression of what the situation is—"

"Her doctor can tell you the facts. I really don't know—"

"I'll get all that. But I'd like the opinion of a friend. That is, if you can spare the time? I realize it's already late."

"Of course I can spare the time," she said.

Again she offered him a smile. A smile like a gift— that's how he used to think of smiles and laughter from her. She'd given him so much, so freely from the heart. Every moment with her had been like discovering something he'd never known he'd missed.

Just seeing her face brought that feeling back.

But then, of course, he strode in to see his sister.

Two

Emma paced the hallway outside Room 201, glancing at her watch every few minutes, thinking that she shouldn't stay. It wasn't as if she were direct family, not to Garrett or Caroline. She had no real business being here. She was just a friend. And she couldn't help feeling awkward because of her history with Garrett.

But then he stumbled out of Caroline's room, and her breath caught just looking at him.

He wasn't that brash, sexy boy she remembered, the one whose kisses made her knees knock, made her pulse zoom, made her feel like a woman for the first time. But damned if the look of him didn't send a crazy rush straight to her hormones.

He'd looked like Keanu Reeves as a boy. He was still tall and lean, still had the dark hair and magnetic eyes.

Wearing an Italian suit and linen shirt, he radiated sophis-
tication—even as rumpled and exhausted as he obviously
was. Even whipped, though, she saw the power in his face,
in his eyes.

Their history suddenly pinched her heart. He'd fiercely
wanted to get out of Eastwick back then—primarily to
escape his overbearing, controlling parents, a problem she
could positively relate to.

She'd wanted to matter more to him, to factor more in
his decisions. And hadn't. It wasn't as simple as escaping
problems for Garrett. He used to wear a T-shirt that said
It's More Fun To Play In The Deep End. And that was him.
He'd never wanted an easy life, didn't expect one. He
wanted to carve his own niche, to take all the risks, to
make a mark with his own name on it.

Emma knew from gossip that he'd gone after his goals
with both resolve and ambition—and never looked back.
Even so, he didn't look so much like a high roller in the
investment world now. Closer up, she could see the
pinched lines around his mouth, the anxiety and worry in
his expression.

"Thanks for waiting," he said.

She matched his subdued tone. "I'm guessing Caroline's
still asleep?"

"She's out for the count. I didn't want to leave
her…but there doesn't seem any point in sitting there
when she's so deeply under. And I have to believe she
needs the rest."

Emma nodded in agreement. "I'm guessing you rushed
out of New York this afternoon? Have you had a chance to
get any dinner?"

He shook his head. "But I don't want to go far. If you don't mind, I just want to talk to you for a couple minutes."

"Sure. The hospital cafeteria is pitiful, but we should be able to scare up a sandwich or something reasonably edible." She realized he didn't want to be farther than running distance from his sister, but it wasn't that hard to persuade him into a quick snack.

The food choices in the cafeteria were as ghastly as she'd promised. The best he could choose was a dry turkey sandwich on dry whole wheat, stale chips, a cup of pitch-black coffee. But Emma coaxed him to carry it outside, away from the sterile hospital smells and sights. Just beyond the side doors was a mini landscaped garden with cement benches in the moonlight.

"Feels good," he admitted, taking one of the benches. Both of them inhaled the fresh air. A security light beamed enough reflection so they weren't sitting in darkness yet felt the freedom of the shadows. Emma could almost see him relax—or try to.

"I keep thinking this is my fault," he confessed. "Caroline called me twice this week. I was busier than hell, got the messages, just planned to call her back when I had time. She never said it was important or critical, but when the hospital called, my heart just seemed to leap in my throat." He sucked in a breath, turned to look at her. "Would you tell me what you know?"

Emma only wished it were more. "I see her quite often—in town or at different functions. We're not as close as sisters, but I've thought of her as a friend for years, Garrett. I'd have hoped she knew she could turn to me. But the only recent trouble I knew she had was with Griff, and that was ages ago."

He nodded, unwrapped the sandwich, sighed at the look of it and then crunched down. "That was my impression, too. That the marriage had healed up. Caroline had told me more than once that they were happier than they'd ever been."

"That's how it looked to everyone. They've been like newlyweds in public. I'm assuming someone told you that he's gone right now. A three- or four-week trip to China, I think someone said. But Caroline never said anything about any trouble since they reconciled."

"Griff always traveled. I thought that was one of the problems between them originally—all his time away from her, overseas." Garrett gulped down another dry bite of sandwich. "I don't think he's been gone like this in a while, though. And it's really rare that he couldn't be reached by phone."

"I'm sure he'll get here as fast as he can."

"Right now the only question that matters is why'd she do this? What could possibly have been so wrong that she'd consider taking her own life?" Garrett bunched up his paper plate and napkin. "If somebody hurt her, I'll find out. Believe me. But right now I don't have the first clue what could have been so bad that she felt driven to do this."

It wasn't a pretty picture, Garrett confronting someone who'd hurt his sister. Emma thought his lean build, elegant suit and urban appearance were misleading. If she were stuck in an alley with a muscle-bound guy versus Garrett, she'd take Garrett anytime. His backbone had always been steel, his character too stubborn to ever back down—even when he should.

"She hasn't been confiding in anyone," Emma said. "We've all asked each other. Everyone wants to help and feels badly. But maybe she'll start talking now that you're home." She hesitated. "I don't want to say anything negative about your parents, but it's been pretty obvious that she hasn't wanted to see them or say anything to them."

"No surprise there."

He didn't say more on that subject, but he didn't have to. Emma knew his parents. His Keatings were similar to her Dearborns. Both families had serious money. Both families push-pulled their offspring to play the dynasty game by their rules.

Garrett had never been sucked in. Not the way Emma knew she had. But she'd stayed single, fought all her parents' efforts to marry her off, as a way of drawing the line on their control. They'd ardently wanted her to marry into a "good family," have offspring to carry on the Dearborn legacy.

Sometimes Emma felt as if Eastwick had a bit in common with medieval castle life. The wealthy crowd she'd grown up with had believed that sex was a commodity, that a "smart" woman made a good match, using any and all tools she had. The women in her pack knew early on that a woman was expected to sexually please a man. It was part of the job—a woman's job to attract and keep the alpha guys in the pack.

Maybe that was the real world. That's what people kept telling her. So many people seemed to think that women prettied up relationships by calling them "love," when reality was survival, and survival for a woman meant nailing the best provider. Sex was a powerful tool for a woman to use to catch the best guy. Friends thought of Emma as naive for believing otherwise. She never argued with them. She just didn't want to live that way. Maybe there was no fairy tale, but she preferred to live alone than invite a sexual relationship where her performance came with a grade attached.

"What?" Garrett asked her. "From the expression on your face, something's on your mind."

She shook her head with a wry smile. Heaven knew why her mind had curved down that road, except that she'd wanted to give Garrett a chance to finish his mini meal in peace. And being with him had provoked memories of that wild, crazy excitement she'd felt with him—nothing to do with grading cards or skills or sex being a commodity. She'd just fiercely wanted him with all her young seventeen-year-old body. But that was a goofy thought path, especially for this moment, when he had so many serious things on his mind. "Where are you staying while you're home?" she asked him.

"With the parents." He sighed. "To be honest, staying there's my last choice in the universe. But at least to start with, I need to get a better picture of what's going on with my sister. They may not be close to Caroline emotionally, but I'm still hoping they have some clue."

"It just won't be restful staying with them?"

"To say the least." He turned, and it was as if he temporarily forgot all his family worries. Not for long but just for that moment, he looked at her face framed in moonlight, her quiet smile. And suddenly there just seemed the two of them alone in their own private universe. "I'm glad I ran into you."

So blunt. So like him. "Likewise. It's good to see you again. Not under these circumstances, but—"

"I've thought of you. So many times." He never dropped his eyes. "I know I hurt you, Emma."

"Yup. You did. But there's been a lot of water under the bridge since then. We were both young."

"I cared. In fact, I loved you." Again his gaze seemed to sweep her face, her hair, her mouth. All of her. "Don't think I didn't. It was never that I wanted to leave you, wanted to hurt you. I was just frustrated and angry at the life I felt forced into here, always at war with my father. I couldn't stay here."

"I understood then and now, Garrett. The hurt's long healed, honestly." She smiled. "To tell you the truth, I think of you, too. Once the hurt healed…they were just good memories. Nothing like that first feeling of being love. is there? It's the kind of memory you can take out on a rainy day and just…enjoy."

"Trust a woman to soften it up. What I remember was a sexual high so damned painful I'm positive I came close to dying from it. All those Friday nights we took a blanket to Silver Point… Remember that? I'd go home and spend the rest of the night in a cold shower."

She laughed. "Yeah, right."

He was smiling, yet his eyebrows suddenly lifted in a curious expression. "You don't believe me?"

"I believe you're full of the devil, no different than you always were." She was a long way from the shy teenager who blushed when a guy tried a little flirting. But somehow the look in Garrett's eyes—the electric energy of being with him again—was putting a hot sizzle in her pulse. She was too physically aware of him for comfort. Quickly, competently, she steered him away from personal topics.

It worked. In fact, it more than worked. As the minutes passed, she felt relieved they'd found a way to talk naturally together again. He obviously needed and wanted to get back to his sister, but these few moments with some fresh air and a little food had eased the taut strain in his expression. He'd so clearly needed to climb off the anxiety train for a bit. So she told him about the current scandal in town—Bunny Baldwin's death, the infamous missing diaries, everyone worrying about what secrets Bunny had known, Jack Cartright being blackmailed and his marrying Lily and how much happiness had come out of that horrible mess in the long run....

She didn't talk long, just enough to fill him in on the town's personalities. The instant he started to look restless, she stood up, and then swiftly so did he.

"I know," she said without his having to speak up. "You're going back to Caroline. And I need to head home and get some sleep."

"I do need to get back upstairs. But for all this catching up, I still didn't take the chance to ask anything about you." Quick as a sliver, he asked, "So—you aren't still on the loose, are you? You in a good marriage?"

"I'm engaged." The instant the words came out of her mouth, she felt a flush of guilt because, damn, she hadn't thought of Reed in hours now. Not that she'd done anything wrong. She hadn't touched Garrett or kissed him or done anything suggestive in any way.

Yet the instant she said *engaged*, his expression immediately changed. It wasn't as if he stopped smiling at her, but...the lights went off. He quickly closed a door on possibilities that, until that instant, she hadn't realized was open.

Yet on her drive back to the art gallery, alone in the dark, she admitted fibbing to herself.

She might not have touched Garrett, but she'd thought about it.

She might not have taken his personal comments seriously, but her heartbeat had been galloping like a young girl's.

She might not have done anything wrong, but her disloyalty to Reed was still real. And wrong.

Most of the time she lived at her parents' house, where she had a private suite of rooms on the second floor. Often enough, though, she worked late at the gallery and then just stayed in town. Tonight it was already too late to drive home, so she let herself in the back door of Color and slipped off her shoes.

Several years before, she'd converted a small anteroom off the first floor into a home away from home. She kept books, cosmetics, several changes of clothes there, but the room had slowly been filling up with the oddest assortment of treasures. A two-centuries-old Chinese desk, candles wrapped in a necklace of amethysts, a white fur rug by the bed, a narrow Louis XIV mirror… She shook her head at the wild assortment often enough. They were things she loved, but they certainly didn't represent any standard decorating style. The silliest of all was a framed sign—Shall We Dance in the Kitchen?—that meant nothing at all, except that sometimes she wished she were that whimsical and romantic. Or that she could be.

Plunking down on the bed, she kicked off her shoes and phoned her parents to let them know she'd be staying in town, then got ready for bed and switched off the light. She was beat, yet somehow she lay there for hours, staring at the film of white curtains whispering in the window. Garrett refused to leave her mind.

It made no sense. He was the wrong man. *Reed* was the right man, the man she was supposed to be marrying. So why couldn't she stop Garrett from haunting every corner of her thoughts?

In the morning, she promised herself, she'd call Reed. First thing. And until then, she mentally slapped herself upside the head and determined to squash her shameful attitude.

At least she tried to.

Garrett hadn't meant to doze off, but he must have. Because when he opened his scratchy eyes, his neck and knees were cramped from sitting in the straight-back chair. The wall clock claimed more than an hour had passed…and his sister's eyes were open.

He lurched out of the chair, exhaustion forgotten, as he picked up Caroline's hand. He hated hospitals. Never knew what to say or do. But one look at his sister—her face as pale as the sheets, and the sad look in her eyes scaring him—and he wanted to shoot someone.

"Garrett." She said his name as if trying to talk through a mouthful of fuzz. Still, her frail voice managed to communicate relief and love at seeing him.

"I'm sorry I didn't call you back. Beyond sorry," he said fiercely. "I don't know why you did this, sis, and I don't care. I'll help you make it right."

She tried to shake her head. The effort seemed to exhaust her. "You can't. But…glad you came." She licked dry lips. "Love you."

"Love you, too. I want you to rest. We don't have to talk about anything until you're ready. I just want you to know that I'm here. I'll be here. And I won't let anyone pressure you about anything, I swear—"

"Garrett…" Her fingers closed weakly around his wrist. "I know you want to help me. But you can't fix this. No one can. I did something…terrible."

She fell asleep before he could ask anything else, before she could try saying anything else. Garrett wasn't used to anything shaking him, but the defeat and fear in his sister's voice rattled him hard. He sat there, worrying up a storm, until a nurse came in and shooed him out.

He'd have battled the nurse—and won—if he thought there was anything further to gain from staying with Caroline. But right then it was obvious she needed rest more than anything. And if he wanted a chance to get to the bottom of his sister's mess, he needed to get some rest himself.

The Keating estate was a short five miles from town, a two-story brick house set on a hillside, with a curved deck and a sculpted sloping lawn. It loomed in the moonlight like a gothic castle. He used his old house key, let himself in the kitchen entrance and immediately stepped out of his shoes, not wanting to wake his parents or any of the household staff.

It struck his ironic sense of humor that he used to tiptoe just like this when he was a teenager sneaking late into the house. One step into the living room and his big toe crashed into a chair leg. That was a déjà vu, too.

Moonlight flooded in the windows, so that once his eyes adjusted he realized his mother had redecorated again. The decor this time seemed to be some French period. Lots of gilt and tassels. Lots of mean furniture legs. Very elegant, if you went for that sort of thing. Garrett didn't, and his toe was stinging like a banshee.

"Garrett!" His father switched on the light from the paneled doors at the stairway.

"Dad." He offered the hug, knowing his father wouldn't think to. "I'm sorry. I didn't mean to wake you."

"You didn't." Merritt wore pajamas, but his iron-gray hair was brushed, his eyes tired but alert. "Your mother and I are both up. Waiting for you. Hoping you'd gotten something out of Caroline that we didn't."

Upstairs, his parents had a mini living room off their sleeping quarters. Whiskey was poured, neat. His mother pecked his cheek, then curled on the couch in the window seat by the bay windows. "I hope you talked to her," Barbara said immediately.

Garrett plunked down on an oversize footstool. He wasn't about to replay his sister's words. "I stayed for a few hours, but she was sleeping deeply."

"I just don't understand why she'd do this to us!"

Garrett didn't expect either parent to ask how he was, how his life was going. The conversation was immediately about them. "Caroline didn't *do* anything to you. She did it to herself."

His mother rubbed her temples as if she were at the end of her rope. "That's the point. That's the exact point. Everyone will talk. Especially with all this scandal about Bunny's death and those diaries... Now there's just more fuel to the gossip fire. People could think we did something, when you know we gave that girl every advantage a daughter could possibly have. I swear, Caroline was selfish from the day she was born—"

"Mom. She's *troubled*. She has to be in major despair over something or she'd never have done this."

"Oh, pfft." Barbara stood up, waving her glass. "She's spoiled and wants attention. Like always. She doesn't think of me or your father. Or our reputation in the community. She has everything she ever wanted in this life, but does she ever think of us?"

Okay. He'd been in his parents' house all of ten minutes and already he wanted to smash a wall. That fast, he remembered why he'd left Eastwick and never looked back.

Later, though, when he lay in bed in the spare room, he recalled how hard it had been to leave his younger sister alone back then. And more than that, how painful it had been to leave Emma.

Right now it just didn't matter if his parents drove him as crazy as they always had. He couldn't leave his sister to the wolves. Until her husband came home from China—and until Garrett was certain she was going to be all right—he was staying here. Which meant he had to find a way to make his business work here for an indefinite period of time.

Before drifting off to sleep, Emma's face whisked into his mind again. Her thick, glossy hair used to swish all the way down her back. Now she wore it shoulder length, but it was still like moonlight on black silk. So raven-dark, so rich, yet with light in every strand. Her soft mouth was as evocative as it had always been. So were those unforgettable eyes, so deep blue they were almost purple. Eyes a guy could get lost in.

God knows he had.

It still puzzled him that she hadn't looked at him like an engaged woman.

And that her classy clothes showed off a successful, poised woman…yet that wasn't how she'd looked at him either.

From the first second their eyes met, he'd suddenly remembered rolling in the grass with her. Stealing kisses after football games. Pressing her up against the locker after school, feeling her breasts against his chest, pretending to be talking about homework. She'd blush and flush and fluster, but then she'd look at him from under those thick black eyelashes. Teasing him. Emma had loved turning him on, loved the power of it, the fun of it, the joy of it. They'd tempted wicked every which way from Sunday. She'd made him hotter than fire—and far more frustrated.

She'd been shy back then, but there'd been no guile to her, no ability to hold back. For sure there'd been no distance. There'd just been all that honest, helpless young-woman heat in her eyes. The dare-you-to-melt-my-bones look. She'd turned him into putty.

And he'd loved dying from all those hard-ons with no release.

But hell and damnation, if she was engaged, how come she'd still looked at him that way? Unguarded, winsome...as if she were dying to feel those feelings again. With a man. With *him.*

You're imagining all this, he told himself—and knew it was true. He was soul-tired, beyond the ability to think clearly. He needed a good night's sleep—and then he needed to concentrate on his sister.

Not on a woman who was already claimed by someone else.

Three

A few mornings later, Emma stood outside Color with a contractor. She'd been running nonstop, organizing her traditional art show in July, when she'd run into a major maintenance problem.

The contractor hiked up his jeans. "Actually, ma'am, the house didn't suddenly start to sink on that side. The problem was likely developing over a long period of time."

"Well, no one noticed it before." Emma wanted to tear out her hair. A maintenance problem certainly wasn't news. Two-hundred-year-old houses regularly developed ghastly ailments. If it wasn't dry rot one year, it was corroded wiring or termites the next. "I just can't have a big mess right now! Can we put off the work until October?"

"Well, I wouldn't, ma'am."

"You call me ma'am one more time and you won't see

October, either," she said crossly, and sighed. "Okay. Let's hear the plan."

"Yeah, well, we're gonna put up new house jacks. Take down your old porch pillars. Reframe pillars around the new house jacks, but hinged, like, so they're accessible. That way we could do this slow, push up that second story a smidgeon at a time. Don't want to crack this pretty foundation, now, do we?"

Emma's eyes narrowed. He was so *twinkly*. "But why did the house decide to sink now?"

"Taking a wild guess now…but probably because the house is older than the hills and then some?"

"Easy for you to joke. You're going to charge me, what, five figures?"

"Yup, in that general ballpark," he confirmed.

And there was the real rotten apple. Her thirtieth birthday was on August thirty-first—so close now, but not close enough to access the trust fund her grandmother had established for her. In the meantime, she knew her parents would float her the money, but there was always a heavy price tag for those *gifts*.

To add to the morning's confusion, Josh chose that moment to poke his head out the back door. "Mrs. Dearborn's on the phone, Emma—"

"If you don't mind, just tell my mom I'll call her back, okay? Thanks—"

She'd barely given the contractor the okay to destroy her spring budget when she noticed a woman pause at the gate of the white picket fence. The woman was so familiar and yet not. Years before, Emma had attended high school with a girl who had curly, waist-length hair; wore wildly unconventional clothes and had an irrepressible rebellious streak. This woman was groomed to the teeth, a grown-up debutante by Eastwick standards in every way, yet there was just something… "Mary?" she called out hesitantly. "Mary Duvall? Is that really you?"

"I was wondering if you'd recognize me," the woman said.

"As if I could ever forget you!" Emma flew across the lawn to whisk open the gate and draw her old friend into a huge hug, the day's frustrations immediately forgotten. "I thought you were still in Europe, living the high life. It's wonderful to see you!"

"You, too, Emma. And God, I could smack you. You're as beautiful as ever, except…" Her old school friend laughed as she noted the bit of clay under Emma's fingernails. "What's this?"

"I volunteer a couple of hours a week at the local grief center, working with the little ones—and I mean really little ones, the pre-K set. I do finger painting with them or drawing or clay. Love it…" She chatted on a moment more, trying to absorb the changes in her old friend. Mary had disappeared right after graduation to go party in Europe. She was an artist, Emma had heard. It was just…unnerving to see her dressed like a dowager going to a tea party when she'd always been so flamboyant and unconventional. "What are you doing in town? Any chance you're back for good?"

"I have no idea how long I'll be here. Right now I'm just here for my grandfather. He's not well. At his age, there aren't a lot of great choices, you know? But he can't be alone, so I'm just going to live with him for a while." Mary motioned to the Colors sign. "The last time I was home, your gallery was just a dream."

"She's still my dream," Emma admitted with a chuckle and then snapped her fingers. "Say, did you bring any work home with you? Anything you'd like me to display? I have a room for local artists, but especially for you, I'd always find a special spot."

"Maybe. I did bring some work with me. I figured I'd be sitting with my grandfather a lot, so I might as well set up an easel while I was home…. In the meantime, what's new with you? Married now, kids or anything?"

"Engaged. To Reed Kelly."

"You're kidding! Reed, the horse breeder? The race-horses—"

"Yup, that's him."

"He was older than us in school, so I didn't know him well, but I always thought he was such a great guy—"

"He is, he is…." Yet Emma felt a sudden odd itch in the middle of her back. Nothing painful. Just as if a mosquito had suddenly nailed her.

She purposefully ignored it and talked a few more minutes with Mary until she had to leave, and heaven knew Emma had mountains of work still waiting for her. Messages had accumulated in her office—three from her mother. A fund-raiser her mother wanted to attend, a ribbon cutting on a new boutique, a reception for a visiting senator. Nothing Emma wanted to do. All, she suspected, that she'd get roped into. Josh was framing a set of canvases in the back room—stealing her favorite job, or so she teased him.

She'd just run outside to accept a delivery from UPS when she spotted Garrett hiking down the walk of the real-estate office across the way. He turned in the direction of her gallery—probably because his car was parked on Maple—yet he seemed to glance in her direction almost instinctively.

His smile was immediate. His stride quickened. By the time he'd crossed the street, she had the oddest sensation that he'd been taking her in, head to toe. As a boy, he'd always had those bedroom eyes—but teenage boys always had their minds on one thing. It was completely different feeling assessed—and appreciated—by a man who knew women, who knew how much fun—and how dangerous— the right kind of chemistry could be.

She wasn't usually self-conscious about her appearance, but this was one of her free days. She'd not only started the morning working with little kids but had also expected to spend the rest of the day with boxes and frames and ladders. Her hair was casually pinned up with a simple enamel clip. She was wearing lipstick and her grandmother's star-sapphire earrings, but that was it for the fussing. Her twills were ancient, her purple shirt too oversize to be flattering. Yet he seemed to think she looked good, because a sexual charge kindled in his eyes.

She felt exactly the same potent charge…and it scraped on her conscience. That first night, she had excuses—his sister was ill, she hadn't seen him in so long, she was tired, all that stuff. But now she knew that sizzle was strong, knew it wasn't right, yet awareness of him still tiptoed up her senses like a wicked secret.

Even so, when she realized that he was obviously headed for her, she did the hospitable thing and met him at the edge of the yard.

"Amazing what riffraff this neighorhood attracts," she teased.

He laughed. "So this is your gallery?"

"Sure is." She hesitated, not wanting to invite trouble but feeling the increasing need to understand why he still had such a tormenting pull for her. "I've got a mountain of stuff to do—bet you do, too—but come in if you have a few minutes. I'll get you a cup of coffee, show you around... How's Caroline?"

He sucked in a breath. "Not great. She's still not talking—but something clearly happened to her. This isn't like a chemical depression. Something specifically had to trigger this, something that's killing her. You haven't heard any gossip in town?"

"Tons of it. But nothing ever about Caroline. Everyone likes her, Garrett. And everyone was hoping she and Griff would get back together when they hit that rough patch." She led him inside. "Has anyone reached her husband yet?"

"They keep trying. Messages have been left at all his contact points, so it's just a matter of him checking in. Deep inside China, communications just aren't what they are here."

Josh poked his head out to say hello. She brought out a mug of java for Garrett, then got trapped on the telephone with a customer. By the time she caught up with him, he'd obviously been freely wandering around. "My God, Emma, what you've made of this place."

His enjoyment buoyed her spirits as nothing else could have, so she couldn't resist showing off some of her favorites. Right inside the lobby was a fish tank—not filled with fish but with a mermaid sculpted in marble and inlaid with precious and semi-precious stones. "I found the artist—and this crazy, wonderful piece—in a tiny jewelry store in upstate New York."

"One of those who-can-believe-it kind of things? She's…riveting. Hard to take your eyes off her."

That was exactly how Emma had always felt. "Come on, I'll whisk you around upstairs."

She didn't have to coax him. Today he was wearing casual chinos, a dark polo. As a teenager, he'd been a work-aholic and a hard-core overachiever yet always friendly and gregarious. He was still easy to talk to, but maturity had given him an inner quietness. His emotions didn't show the way they used to. He had that mover-and-shaker look, that kind of virile, vital energy, even with his emotions locked out of sight. She wondered—she hoped—that he'd found someone to love him. Really love him. Because he seemed vitally alone.

Beware, whispered her hormones.

But she *was* aware now and had every intention of being careful.

Surely it wasn't wrong to feel compassion for him, though. His sister was in the middle of a frightening crisis, after all.

She showed him her Oriental lacquer room and the long, skinny hall where she displayed a range of Oriental carpets. She reserved the far east room for women's art—sculptures, oils, watercolors, cameos of women in all shapes and forms. The west room across the hall echoed a range of art about males—men sleeping, studying, working, fighting, enjoying guy hobbies. Down a few doors was her "room of light," which displayed work with gems.

"Sheesh, Emma. You've put together the most unique gallery I've ever seen," he said. "The way you present everything is just…fun. But it's also thoughtful and interesting."

"Quit being so nice. It's going to my head." But damn, it was nice to share her love. She'd put a ton of thought into every room, every piece she used for display, every artist she chose to represent. "Hey, you haven't said what you were doing at the real-estate office. You suddenly thinking about buying property in Eastwick?"

"When hell freezes over," he said wryly, but he motioned to the sheaf of papers under his arm. "I picked up a list of short-term rentals from the agent."

"I thought you'd planned to stay home?"

"So did I." His tone was rueful. "I should have known that wouldn't work. But now that I've been around Caroline, talked to her doctors, I'm afraid I'm going to be here for a while. At least a few weeks."

"Oh, Garrett. You're that worried your sister isn't going to recover from this?"

"I just don't know. In fact, *all* I know is that I can't leave her. And I'll likely get on better with my parents if I'm not under their feet—and they're not under mine." He walked into the upstairs bathroom—just to see what she'd done in there, as if he knew she'd done *something*. And she had. The ceiling was a mural of graphic comic art, all superheroes. He came out chuckling—and claiming to have a crook in his neck—but he pretty swiftly returned to their conversation.

"Anyway…I decided I'd better look for some alternative living arrangement. So far, though, I'm not thrilled with the places the real-estate agent came up with. All of them are a distance from town. I don't want that, don't want to stay in a hotel either. It's easy enough for me to fly or helicopter into New York several times a week. All I need is a simple place to set up a temporary office. A bed, a mini kitchen. Some quiet. A place to set up a computer, fax, printer, that sort of thing. I don't want anything fancy or far."

She frowned thoughtfully as she led him back downstairs. "If you want a place in town, I actually know of one. Just two doors down, in fact."

Garrett raised an eyebrow. "The agent claimed there was nothing close in town."

"That's because it's not on the formal market." She explained the situation. Most of the old homes on the block used to be residential, but they'd been gradually turning into businesses—lawyers, accountants, psychologists, brokers, that kind of thing. Not the kind of commerce that required big parking needs, but quiet enterprises that were willing to maintain the historical flavor of the buildings. "Anyway, my neighbor, Marietta Collins, is a holdout. She rented her upstairs to a boarder, a writer, only he recently moved. She didn't list it because she only wants to rent to friends of friends. I have no idea what the place looks like, Garrett, so maybe it won't suit you at all. But if you like, I could call her…"

He did like. It only took Emma a second to dial and find out the place was still available for rent. Garrett blinked at the price.

"I can't imagine why she's giving it away."

"Well, it could be a clunker. But I think she just really wants someone she can trust living above her."

"Good thing you had pull, huh?" From the amused

sparkle in his eyes, Garrett was obviously not used to anyone having to pull strings for him—likely it was usually the other way around.

"Well, you'd better see it before you get your hopes up. You might decide the real-estate agent had better ideas for you."

"There really isn't much to rent. You know how Eastwick is. Everyone wants to own. And no one's looking to encourage transients."

She had to laugh at the idea of Garrett being considered a transient. And though he expressed concern over stealing any more of her workday, she walked over to the place with him. She knew Marietta would be uneasy without a personal introduction—and she was also a little worried what she might have gotten him into. If the place was a disaster, she didn't want him to feel obligated to take it because of her.

Marrietta Collins took one look at Garrett, beamed and promptly gave them the key to check out the upstairs at their leisure.

Emma's impression of the apartment was the opposite of Garrett's. "Well, it isn't exactly a garret, Garrett, but—"

"That pun is sick. I've always liked a sick sense of humor in a woman."

She had to chuckle—but the apartment was hardly what Garrett must be used to. A few centuries before, the structure had been a tavern where customers slept upstairs—apparently next to each other, since there was only one main room. Obviously the details had been modernized, but the core architecture had been preserved. The mellow old floorboards creaked and groaned, but they'd obviously been treasured, because they were polished to a high gleam. Honey-pine paneling framed a small stone fireplace. The bathroom was strictly utilitarian, but the tiny kitchen area had an eating nook tucked under a graceful Palladian window, shaded by giant elms just outside.

"The furniture's the pits," Emma said ruefully.

Garrett was checking out every window view. "Spoken like a woman," he teased. "There's a couch and a chair. What more do I need?"

"Some lamps. Some pictures. Some rugs," she fussed.

"It's got a decent desk." He motioned to the relic that may—*may*—have been a teacher's desk in some century past. Emma loved antiques, but in this case she thought someone should have had the sense to throw it out—in that same century past.

"I guess I just assumed there'd be a separate bedroom." Instead a double bed was tucked in a side alcove, slanted under the eaves.

"This way there'll be lots of airflow. Ideal in the summer."

She checked out the kitchen, since he didn't seem interested in opening drawers and cupboards there. "It's ultraclean. Which is good. But there isn't a single plate or dish. No pans. Not even a single set of silverware."

"Dishes. Who wants dishes? The place has outlets. Lots of outlets." He bounced back to his feet after examining the location of all the electrical plugs. "No sweat setting up a system here. And the windows are great. Lots of light."

She shook her head. There was lots of light because the windows were bald of any curtains or shades—but Garrett was happier than a kid at the circus. Who could fathom men? He was used to money. Big money. Nice things, conveniences. "Well, it wouldn't take too much to make it at least livable. And it really is pretty nice for the price—"

"Nice? *Nice?* I was prepared to pitch a tent. This is better than a dream."

The lunatic jogged over to her, making her laugh…until she saw something unexpected in his eyes. Maybe he hadn't given in to a foolish, exuberant impulse in so long that he'd forgotten what it was like. She wasn't absolutely positive he even knew he was going to kiss her.

But she knew before he was halfway across the room. High-powered men had high-powered drives. Sometimes the release valve slipped open when it shouldn't. And debutantes raised in Eastwick weren't soft; they only looked that way. Emma knew what was happening, knew how to get out of a problem like this gracefully.

And that was what she intended—to carefully duck away from him. But he swooped down on her with none of the finesse and skill and technique she remembered. He was just a guy high on life for that instant. Just a guy with a goofy smile on his face, swinging his girl around in a circle to make her squeal…just a little happiness letting loose, nothing dangerous, nothing wicked.

The feeling of his long, strong arms wrapping around her triggered…something. A stillness deep inside her. She suddenly wasn't laughing—or squealing. Instead her lips tilted up to meet his, as if that were the only choice she had. The only choice she'd ever had.

Suddenly the only sound in the room was the sweet June wind whispering in the open window. He took her mouth as if he were desperate for the taste of her. She molded close, as if she were desperate to be held, not by someone, not by a man, but specifically, oh so specifically, by him. The taste of him created a fierce, strong pull deep in her belly.

She lost her balance. He found it. She lost her senses, and he stole those, too, lifting his head, searching her eyes with one long, still moment…and then going back for another kiss. This time with the gloves off.

Tongue found tongue. Teeth found teeth. His hands held her head still, then, impatient, pulled at the clip trapping her hair. Her hair spilled free, through his fingers. She wrapped her hands around his wrist, but it didn't slow him down, didn't stop him. Didn't seem to stop her either.

As if her breasts had never known a man, their tips tightened and hardened, yet she pressed closer. They both began a dance of intimacy—a dance without music yet so about rhythm, so about the sway of breast to muscle, of soft pelvis to turgid erection. The drift of her scent waltzed to the scent of his soap, his skin, him. Another dip, another kiss, and her heart picked up a faster rhythm now, as if he'd suddenly spun her into a tango until she couldn't catch her breath. His breath, his kisses, the strength of his hips, pressed against hers, enticed her to move with him, to want him.

Want.

What a word for a woman who'd had no time for sex, who was impatient at the whole idea of how much importance everyone else put on sex. Who just wanted to live her life with passion for all the wonderful things life offered but not for passion.

Okay, she kept telling herself. *Okay. This is some kind of aberration. Ghosts* aren't *real. Hallucinations aren't real.* He was terribly stressed, she figured. That was all this was really about. He'd always been a workaholic beyond all sanity, so then he'd come home and been terribly worried about his sister—and he'd never been a guy who tolerated frustration well.

Yeah. That was it. He was just letting off steam with these kisses.

Only she wasn't. She didn't have steam to let off. This…clinging to him. This wildly, fiercely kissing him back. This teasing him, rubbing against him….none of this made sense. It wasn't her.

This wasn't sex. This was heart-altering. This wasn't passion. It was touching at some other level. Down, down, down at the deep, sad loneliness level. Damn it, she hadn't been lonely in all this time. She *hadn't*.

Yet he made her feel that way.

As if she'd been alone since they'd last kissed as teenagers. As if she'd needed no one until this moment. As if she'd been coping fine—which she had, she *had*—until Garrett came home and took her mouth this way and made it all come crumbling down.

She felt his hands soothing down her back, seducing with every rub, every caress. His mouth still took more kisses, took ownership of her senses. He spun her around, pressed her against a honey-pine wall. The rough pine felt good against her spine, a relief after that dangerous silk mouth of his. His hands roamed her arms now, then whispered between them, reaching for her blouse buttons.

Her eyes shot open.

He hadn't felt her bare breasts yet. They hadn't removed any clothes. But a couple minutes more of this, and Emma would have peeled down without his asking. Without any talk. Without her thinking even once of her fiancé.

She broke away, slid out from under his arms, looked at him—stricken—and then shot out the door and down the stairs.

Four

At first the sky only dribbled down, but in a matter of minutes the rain turned into a flushing downpour. Emma flicked the windshield wipers on high, but they couldn't keep up. The windows started to steam. Thankfully Reed's place was only a few more miles, because she could barely see.

Her nerves echoed the snap of lightning as she finally reached the sign for Rosedale Farms.

She had to see her fiancé. Now. This afternoon.

The embrace she'd shared with Garrett was still glued on her mind—and heart. It was wrong in every way to have kissed another man when she was engaged. And worse than that—much, much worse—was realizing she'd responded to Garrett more honestly and passionately than she'd ever responded to Reed.

She'd assumed the old sizzle she'd once felt for Garrett

was the stuff of young hormones and first love—the kind of thing a woman outgrew. She honestly didn't know she had that kind of sexuality or sensuality in her. Didn't know life even held that possibility for her. And she had no idea what all these feelings for Garrett meant, if anything. But right now wasn't the time to deal with that.

Right now what she absolutely had to deal with was facing Reed. There was no more denying that something was gravely, fundamentally wrong with their relationship. Maybe she'd realized before that they hardly had a grand passion for each other, but not that they were missing something critically elemental.

Her whole world felt shaken. She kept telling herself that a few kisses from an old love shouldn't have the power to upend her life. But reality was more that seeing Garrett again had forced open old, carefully locked emotional doors. She'd never meant to lie to herself, but it seemed she had.

Anxiety thrummed in her pulse. She'd never deliberately run from trouble or responsibility. Her mother had taught her that. Her mom, for as long as Emma could remember, had sneaked little nips all through the day "just to take the edge off." Emma remembered her childhood as nonstop tip-toeing, trying to be quiet for her mother, trying not to give her mom yet another reason to take one of those infernal nips. So no, Emma was a long way from perfect. She did things wrong, made mistakes, sometimes bad mistakes.

But at least she didn't run.

Yeah, right, she thought wryly as she braked in front of the stables. Her heart was thumping louder than thunder. Everywhere she looked there were tons of vehicles—the big house always had a bunch of cars parked outside, and this afternoon, with the rain, the barns and stables had pickups of all sizes and shapes lined up like a parking lot.

Rosedale had been named after Reed's grandmother, and although Reed ran the whole kit and caboodle, his entire family was involved. And needed to be. The Kellys did everything related to horses—boarding, foaling, bloodstock management. Reed owned and trained a number of racehorses, as well, and he kept a full roster of pedigreed stallions available for stud service. The place was always packed.

In principle, Emma loved riding. But in reality she'd only done it three times because she'd fallen off all three times—a running joke between her and Reed, given his business. The point, though, was that all those cars and trucks meant he was busy. Still, Reed was always busy at this time of year, so if she wanted to talk to him, she had to track him down here and see if he could steal a few minutes.

There was no way she could break it off with him on the phone—nor would she ever have chosen that coward's way out.

She climbed out of the car and dashed for the stable office—her first best bet at finding him. Rain soaked through her pale blue shirt and pants, but it was a warm enough rain. She was inside in seconds. Horsey smells immediately rushed her nostrils—hay and horseflesh and leather and liniment and you-know-what. Truthfully she'd always liked the smells—even the you-know-what. Just because horses never liked her didn't mean she wasn't fond of them.

Today, though, her stomach roiled the minute she stepped in—not because of the smell, but because she immediately heard the crazed sounds from the far end of the stable. She knew what the sounds were, knew what they meant. A mare was being mounted by a stallion—a force-feed situation that Reed was invariably directly involved in, because an ardent stallion could, and often did, hurt a mare if humans didn't direct the activity. Harnesses and pulleys and lifts and all kinds of unlikely things were used to aid an advantageous mating. Emma got it. Advantageous marriages were a big deal in high society, no different. But if there was anything unromantic in this life, it was a mare and stallion get-together.

Instantly she realized that she'd been an idiot to come without calling—and a selfish idiot besides. Reed had never minded an impromptu visit from her, but this was different. She wasn't just visiting. This panicked rush to see him was absurd. It wasn't as if anything had to be settled that very second. It was guilt driving her, not really need.

Before she could turn around, Reed spotted her and separated himself from the clutch of people near the breeding station.

"Emma!"

Oh, God. His face lit up with a welcoming smile, as if she hadn't obviously crashed his busy day. "What a great surprise," he said and swooped down for a hug—then stopped with a sheepish grin. He *did* smell like horse and man sweat—and eau de stable in general. It was one of the things she loved about Reed, his consideration for her. But right then she didn't care. She wanted a hug from her fiancé.

She wanted, needed, some kind of proof that she was crazy. If she could just feel something solid for him—with him—maybe she could talk herself out of breaking this off.

She forced a warm smile. "I can see I picked the worst moment in the universe to see you. You're busier than a one-armed bandit."

"And with one of your favorite things. But His Highness finally decided to perform, so I believe we can sneak away from the unwilling lovebirds—"

Over his shoulder she could see at least two people turn in his direction as if wanting to ask him a question. "Darn it," she said. "I really did pick a rotten time. I should have called."

"I'd rather see you than do business anytime. But what's wrong?" He steered her toward the stable office, which wasn't far, but at least it was a little distant from all the prying eyes. Reed, being Irish, had a cast of thousands in his family—all of whom she loved a bunch. They were warm, gregarious, effusive people, exactly the opposite of her quiet, ultraprivate family. But they were also nosy. And Reed led his business the same way—like a family, with anyone who came by treated to a cup of joe in the kitchen, no fanfare and no airs.

"Come on, I can see something's on your mind. Spill it," he urged her. Typically his stable office resembled the aftermath of a cyclone. The phone had three active lines, the mini fridge was always stocked with pop and bottled water and his desk was heaped with horse bandages, racing schedules, worm shots and every other thing.

She touched her fingers to her temples. He talked so easily. For her, it always took effort. "Reed, I just feel that we should—"

The phone rang. He made a motion begging for patience, hooked the receiver in his ear and served her a pop at the same time. There was a mix-up in some training schedule. He leaned against the desk while motioning her to take the one and only seat—an old leather chair meant for a man to crash for a few minutes with his feet up.

She couldn't sit. She waited, looking at this man she'd agreed to marry more than a year ago. She'd known him forever. He had those Irish looks—the brown hair, the clean skin, the mischievous smile. As a kid, he'd been good-looking in a fresh, clean-cut way, but at thirty-five, he'd come into his own. There was kindness in his character, an easy way with people. No amount of chaos ever seemed to throw him. His judgment—as far as horses and business both—had turned the family horse farm into a highly prosperous enterprise.

Emma felt the knot tie tighter in her stomach. She loved him. For real. There was really no doubt in her mind of that. No one could *not* love Reed. He was an absolutely super man. Good to the bone. A man you could trust through thick and thin. A family man.

What was not to love?

"Okay," he said when he clicked off the phone. "You've got my full attention."

She took a breath. Outside, she heard a rumble of an engine—like an eighteen-wheeler driving in. Voices zoomed past the stable office door. A horse whinnied. It was like trying to think in the middle of a tornado.

She took a breath, then gave up. "Reed, this is no place to talk. I'll just—"

"It's okay, it's okay." He pushed the door, which didn't completely close but at least created a little privacy barrier. Then he lifted his phone. "I'm turning off both the pager and the phone right now—"

But not before the phone rang again. He fielded that call quickly and impatiently. Then did just what he'd said— turned it off and tuned out all the other interruptions, as well. He looked at her intently. "I know what this is about. Your mother called me."

"My mother—?"

"Apparently she thinks you don't want to go to some shindig at the country club on Saturday. The formal June dance? So she talked me into promising to go. I know, I know, I should have asked you. Especially if you wanted out of that darn thing. But damn, she's going to be my mother-in-law, so when she twisted my arm, I couldn't very well turn her down—"

"I understand. No, no, it's not about that."

"All right," he said curiously and leaned back against the desk, his attitude one of waiting, as if determined to give her all the time she needed to say whatever she needed to.

But she heard another major commotion outside—as if a truck had arrived and was being unloaded. This was going nowhere. Yet Emma tried, blurting out, "Reed…do you realize how many times we've postponed setting a date for the wedding?"

"So that's what this is about. And you're right. So right. In fact, Weddings By Felicity called me. I don't mean Felicity—it was one of her assistants, Rita someone…"

Emma tried to open her mouth to interrupt, but he lifted a hand.

"It's my fault about that, Emma. I know Felicity is your friend and she seems like a great person besides. But she's justifiably ticked at us for not setting a date, especially this late in the game."

"The thing is," Emma tried to interject, "I think there's a reason we've waited so long—"

"I do, too. Your gallery has the July show coming up. And I'm busier than a magpie here. And since we're doing the ceremony at your parents' house, it didn't seem like all that much had to be completely pinned down, you know? I mean, we didn't have to book a hall, and the photographer and master chef are already in the family, so what difference did it make if it was the second or third Saturday in August?"

"Reed…I think the reason for our procrastinating is more complicated than that."

He nodded again. "Yeah, I know. Truth is—and I know it's selfish—but I get antsy anywhere near a big wedding. Call it a guy thing. Hell, it isn't the party part of it I mind. You know that. With my clan, they'd have a party every Saturday night if we could all survive the hangovers on Sunday morning. But it's the society part of it that makes me squirm. Now that Bunny's gone and no one's stepped up to do that *Eastwick Social Diary* anymore, maybe people won't make so much of every wedding, but…"

"Reed, I've always agreed with you on that. I never wanted a big wedding, either. But once my parents got involved, it was like budging two elephants." Somehow she found her hand on her stomach again, pressing hard to quell the sick, sad feeling inside. "I postponed deciding on a wedding date as many times as you have."

"And that's the thing. We've both been running faster than rats in a maze. If we could just steal a solid blink of time together, we could surely get a date down in ink."

"Yes, I'm sure we could. But the question is…is that

what we want to do? I'm not so positive that it's just busyness that made us both postpone nailing down a wedding date for so long."

He didn't look hurt. He didn't look concerned. He didn't look as if he were remotely getting her at all. "Emma, you know I tend to do better if you just say flat out what's on your mind. I don't know what you mean—"

A beanpole kid jammed a hand through the doorway. "Mr. Kelly. Pretty Lady, they said she leaped the fence in the east pasture, taking off after Wild Wind."

"Aw, hell." Reed startled straight, grabbed his hat from the desk and then looked frantically at Emma.

"No, it's okay. Go. We'll talk later—"

"You come first, Emma. You know that. But damn it—"

"I know, I know. We'll talk on Saturday night if we can't catch each other before. Go, go, I can see this is important."

She really could. Yet on the ride home, the sky was still sending down blistering torrents of rain, echoing the moody restlessness in her heart.

She'd handled that all wrong. Barging in on his work day. Trying to talk about something serious with all that chaos going on. And it wasn't as if she had to hurry into this conversation—she didn't want to hurt Reed. In fact, she'd hoped terribly, desperately, that seeing him would make Garrett fade from her mind, would make her remember all the reasons she'd agreed to this engagement.

But it seemed that goal had boomeranged on her, because she *did* remember why she'd accepted his ring. The reasons were still there, still real. They got on as easily as old slippers. They were both tired of people pushing them into marriage. They both had long ties to Eastwick.

She adored his family, respected his work and his dreams. He totally respected her gallery, her goals, the things she wanted to do; in fact, she couldn't imagine Reed interfering with anything she ever said she wanted.

Yet when she catalogued all those reasons in her mind, the problem was still there.

The idea of marrying Reed was increasingly giving her panicked, shooting headaches and itchy hives. Maybe she loved him…but not in the right way. It was Garrett, damn him, who'd made her realize the heart full of emotions she was missing. The longing she yearned for. The desiring and being desired that her woman's soul whispered for. The feeling of belonging…

She'd never had those feelings in her life. Growing up. Ever. Who knew if it could even happen?

But she knew positively that she didn't have those feelings with Reed.

Halfway home, she hit a red light at Whitaker. She suddenly started crying. Her. Emma Dearborn. Who hadn't cried even when she'd broken an ankle in second grade.

But it was damn scary to realize you had your life all planned in tidy little lines, and suddenly someone was making you color with no lines at all.

Garrett pushed open the door to the hospital, wishing he could shake off like a puppy. The rain had turned into a downright soppy deluge. He'd be dripping less if he ever remembered to carry an umbrella, but that was a nonstarter, never going to happen. The afternoon threatened to turn into pure wet steam—which matched his mood all too well.

The last few days had been more frustrating than finding a mosquito in the dark. Setting up a temporary office and living quarters in Eastwick had been easy enough, thanks to Emma. But his sister's problems relentlessly preyed on his mind.

He'd been interviewing anyone in Eastwick who was willing to talk to him—at least, anyone who knew Caroline. And it seemed as though most of the town did and was willing to talk. Only no one seemed to have a clue about her private life. This morning turned into a total zero.

He'd started out talking with Lily Cartright. She was a sweetheart and a half and a true-blue honest kind of woman. But when he'd asked to have coffee with her, he hadn't realized she'd be as big as a whale. She'd claimed she was going to have a baby in a few months. He figured she was having three at least. But the point was, like everyone else, Lily was troubled about Caroline—but knew nothing.

Then he'd tried Vanessa Thorpe, another of his sister's friends. Because she'd married a rich, older man, the scandalmongers tsk-tsked behind her back. Garrett couldn't care less about gossip or her personal life. He'd just hoped she knew something, anything, about Caroline—but he'd struck out there, too.

After that, he'd tracked down a couple of men. Frank Forrester had to be seventy, not a contemporary of Caroline's, but because he was such a fixture at Eastwick's country club, Garrett thought he'd be a great source of information. He was, but not about Caroline.

Harry, the bartender at the Emerald Room, knew everyone's secrets and then some, but he was genetically related to a clam. Still, he swore he'd have told Garrett something about his sister's health if he'd known anything.

Bottom line was that lots of people thought the world of Caroline, but no one had the smallest inkling what had provoked her sudden depression. Garrett handled frustration as well as he handled fine china—which was a not. He also knew that fear for his sister wasn't the only thing riding his mood.

Emma was.

He hadn't seen her in several days now. Between trying to run his business long-distance and tracking down leads on his sister, he'd had no time to casually run into her. But shame had been riding his conscience, and he hated the feeling.

God knows he had faults, Garrett thought as he loosened his collar in the stifling elevator. He was selfish, singularly directed. He didn't play life by softball rules, never wasted time playing touch-tackle type of football either. He played to win. A lot of people called him stone-headed, a workaholic—but women always claimed he was just as relentless in the sack, a great lover.

And that was good, he mused, except that he knew he was lousy when it came to remembering to call later. In fact, his name was jut plain absentee in the longterm-relationship column.

The bug in his soup, though, was that he'd never had a woman run away from him—not the way Emma had run out the other day.

Nor had a woman ever come alive, come apart in his arms. Not the way she had.

He didn't come on to women who were taken. Ever. Poaching wasn't his thing. Ever. Only, for Pete's sake, what the hell was Emma doing responding to him as if she were the loneliest, hottest woman ever born, if she was happily in love with some guy?

It didn't add up.

"Garrett!"

Just in case he needed more trouble today, fate suddenly produced his mother hustling toward him, coming out of Caroline's hospital room. His mom, typically, looked dressed for tea at the White House, lots of cream and pearls and scented from head to toe with the signature perfume some fancy chemist had created for her.

"I'm so, so glad I caught up with you, dear." His mother hooked his arm and firmly steered him toward a quiet alcove, away from the rooms and nursing station. "I assume you're here to see Caroline and I want to talk to you first."

"How's she doing?"

His mother looked past his shoulder, ensuring no one was within earshot. "The doctor put her on some kind of antianxiety medicine. Insisted on her seeing another psychiatrist."

Garrett frowned. "You think that's wrong?"

"Garrett." His mother rolled her eyes. "*Depression* is such a buzzword for your generation. Everyone has tough stretches in life. That's no excuse to curl up in a bed—or take drugs. I didn't raise either you or your sister to be weaklings."

He struggled for patience. He'd realized years ago that his mother wasn't as cold as she came across. She'd just fought hard to live the good life—as she defined it—and feared anything that was a threat to that. "Mom," he toned down his voice, "depression isn't a character weakness. It's an illness. Being mad at Caroline for this is like being mad at someone for getting cancer."

"She doesn't have cancer. She's healthy as a horse. She's been through dozens of tests. And that's the point. There is *nothing* wrong with that girl, nothing keeping her in bed all this time. Your father and I are at our wits' end."

Okay. No way to open doors in that direction, so he tried another. "Has anyone been able to reach Griff yet?"

"Oh, yes. Your father finally connected with him last night—in the middle of the night, in fact. Our embassy, their embassy, on and on, it took forever. We didn't *get* him, but he's been located now. It could take as long as a week before he's home, but at least we know he's coming."

"That's good—"

"*Exactly.* I drove straight to the hospital to tell Caroline that Griff was coming home, thinking that would finally perk her up. Instead she started sobbing. Crying so loud, they ended up having to sedate her." Finally she lost steam on that subject, only to start up another. "Garrett, I want you to come to the club on Saturday night. There's a dance. The annual June gala—"

"Thanks, Mom. But I'd rather join a chain gang in Siberia." There. He almost won a smile…but not quite.

"Now don't be difficult. We need you there. We need to stand together as a united family."

He scratched his chin. "Honest to Pete, who the hell cares if we're a united family?"

"Everyone. This entire community will notice if we're not there. And the thing is, your sister will be the one to suffer if people start to think she's mentally…unbalanced."

"Some people are going to judge no matter what we say or do—but nobody I'd want to be around. And no one I'd want Caroline around either. So I can't imagine why that matters."

"Garrett, I know you don't share the same values that your father and I do. But your sister loves the club. She has so many friends there. When she comes to her senses, she's going to want to go back, to events just like this. So this is for her, not for you—"

"All right, all right, I'll go."

His mother was just starting to wind up, but now she squinted at him in surprise. "You'll go?"

"Yup. Just tell me what time."

"It's black-tie," his mother warned him.

Well, hell and double hell. But somewhere in those massive closets in the mansion, Garrett knew his mom had saved both a white and a black tux. It wasn't as if he hadn't been roped into those neck-choking functions a zillion times before.

Once his mother left, he sat with Caroline for another hour. She never woke up enough to talk, apparently because of the fresh sedation they'd given her. But she squeezed his hand…which made his heart climb straight into his throat.

No matter how much torture the club dance was, he was more than happy to attend. Hearing that the country club was a nest of Caroline's friends was the impetus. Someone there was going to know something. He'd asked everyone else he could think of, but obviously he didn't know all her acquaintances because he hadn't hung out in Eastwick for years.

As he headed back to his rented apartment, frustration

and worry climbed his mood. So far he'd completely failed the course in helping his sister.

He wasn't used to failure. For damn sure, he wasn't used to feeling helpless. Maybe getting some work done would at least clear his mind. Only he'd barely parked the car and climbed out before he saw the new crisis waiting for him.

This particular crisis was wearing a silver-blue T-shirt that gloved her breasts like a faithful lover, a white skirt that looked thin as a handkerchief and a glisten of careless sapphires in the bangle on her wrist.

Oh, yeah. And she had eyes softer than violets.

For two days he'd almost—almost—forgotten that.

Five

Garrett knew he'd see Emma again—that was a guarantee in Eastwick—but he'd counted on some warning. Some time to prepare. Some space to remember that he was a mature, successful adult instead of a teenager wired on hormones and lust.

Well, he *did* have a couple of seconds, because he spotted her before she spotted him.

She was at the top of the outside back stairs. He'd started using that back entrance because it was private and he didn't have to go through his landlady's house. But why-ever and whatever Emma was doing there initially eluded him. When he climbed halfway up the stairs, he saw that she'd apparently been piling boxes and sacks against his back door. And then she turned.

"Well, if you aren't a sight for sore eyes after a mighty long day. But what is all this?" He motioned to the boxes.

She'd heard him. He knew she'd heard him. But for that instant when their eyes met, she went totally still, as if her heart had stopped beating. And damned if his didn't stop, too.

Her face looked sun-kissed, her mouth bare, her eyes so vulnerable. The T-shirt made her breasts look soft and round and touchable. The pale summer skirt looked as if it'd strip off fast. Evocatively fast. Seductively fast. One look, and all he could think about was claiming her.

"I…" Quickly her expression changed. She smiled, found her poise again. "It's been bugging me, about your being stuck camping out in this bald apartment. I always have spare things sitting around the gallery. And it's June right now, so I'm getting ready for a particularly big show in July, which means I'm even more crowded. So I just figured you might be able to use a few things to make the place more comfortable."

She lifted some items so he could see the nature of the stuff she'd brought over. A pair of Walter Farndon prints of sailboats—as if she could have known he was nuts for sailboats. A stone sculpture in lapis. A bright woven *mola.* A couple giant-size blue bath towels. A woven basket with some basic kitchenware—a few white plates, white bowls, silverware, mugs with bulls and elephants on them.

Some of the items were undoubtedly from her gallery. But not all.

He looked at her.

Emma rarely showed nerves, yet she suddenly tugged on an earring. "You don't have to take a thing. If something's not to your taste, don't sweat it in any way…."

He kept looking at her.

"But I'm just two doors down, so it was kind of silly not to offer you the use of some things that might perk up the place, make you feel more comfortable away from home…"

He kept looking at her.

And finally the puff seemed to go out of her sails. She sank down on the top step, which left just enough room for him to hunker down next to her. The air was humid enough to wear. Even though the rain had finally stopped, leaves and branches hung heavy with moisture, dripping, catching the late-afternoon sunlight. A pair of rowdy peony bushes clustered under the fence, untended and out of control, yet the scent of the flowers wafted up, so delicate they'd catch your breath.

Or else, she was the one catching his breath.

"This was really nice of you," he said quietly. "But you didn't take time out of a workday just to make this apartment more livable."

She hesitated, then lifted her hands in a humorous gesture of defeat. "Darn it, I can fib to most people without getting caught. How come you're so hard to fool? But you're right. I admit it. I needed to do this."

"You needed to do exactly what? Bring this stuff?" He motioned. "Which really is appreciated by the way. I've been camping out with no problem. But damn, it *is* pretty bald in there."

She nodded. "Honestly, I thought a few additions would help. But that was just my excuse for coming over. The truth is that I needed to see you."

"Needed." He repeated the word, unsure why she'd chosen it or what it meant.

She pulled up her knees, tugged her skirt down, tucked a strand of hair behind her ears. And suddenly she no longer looked like the coolly elegant, poised gallery owner, but the predebutante girl he'd once been so head over heels for.

"It's been on my mind. The way I ran off the other day," she admitted. "Darn it, I haven't done anything that cowardly since I can remember."

He wasn't going to haul off and kiss her. Maybe he couldn't stop thinking about it, but that didn't mean he was going to *do* it. "That's funny. I didn't see anything that looked like cowardice. What I saw was a woman who seemed pretty shook up. But then, so was I. Lady, can you ever kiss."

Her cheeks suddenly bloomed with color brighter than all those peonies. "Well, that was exactly the problem. Not how I kissed. But how *you* kissed, buster."

"Yeah, I like your version of the story better. It's just too tough on my male ego to admit that a woman knocked my socks off, especially with nothing more than a few kisses. Much easier to swallow that my expertise and sex appeal threw you. Although, I have to say, I've never scared a woman into galloping out of sight at the speed of sound before."

A sound escaped her throat. A tickle of a chuckle. "Quit it. You're making me feel better. And I know perfectly well I behaved like a goose."

"You know what? I'm almost positive we can both survive an awkward moment."

"I know we can. We're not kids anymore. It's just…it would have been awkward." She lifted a hand in a universally female gesture. "So I wanted it out in the open. A chance to say I'm sorry that happened, it won't happen again. So you wouldn't have to worry about running into me again, either."

"Okay. Got that off both our chests," he said.

"Right."

"Neither of us is worried about it anymore," he said.

"Right."

And cats danced, he thought. His pulse was pounding like a lonesome stallion near the prettiest filly. He wasn't a nice man. He knew that. Being nice had never been on his most-wanted-attributes list, but all the same, he was usually a more decent guy than this. The problem was sitting so close to her. Seeing the late sunlight catch in the little swoop of hair that brushed her forehead. Seeing her arms wrapped around her knees like a girl's. Seeing those sensual violet-blue eyes trying so hard—too hard—not to look at him.

"Tell me about this guy you're engaged to," he said.

"Reed? Reed Kelly—you know, Rosedale Farms."

"Yeah, of course. He was ahead of me by a year in school. But I just didn't know him well. Seemed like a good guy."

"He is. Couldn't be better. He's got a big, wonderful, gregarious family. He's terrific with kids, with horses. He's kind. Patient…"

"How'd you get together?"

She chuckled, but it wasn't a humorous sound. Suddenly she was pulling at her earlobe again. "My parents have been on my case to marry for years. Produce grandchildren. You know how that goes—"

"Yeah, I do."

"And I was so sick of being the extra woman at dinner

parties and gatherings. Felt like meat being paraded in front of butchers for them to choose the prime cut. Eastwick can be wonderful, but it's not easy to be single in this town. And Reed was getting it from the other end— he was the extra man every time a hostess needed one. Hated it as much as I did. And then at a dinner party, we found ourselves together—the token singles. It was funny, really. We started going to different functions just to save ourselves being set up."

"And you found you clicked."

"I don't know about *clicked*. But he was so easy to be with."

"Easy to be with," Garrett echoed and stood. Huge holes seemed missing in this picture. For one thing, he couldn't fathom how a woman as warm and vibrant as Emma hadn't been tempted by marriage long before this. And granted, he would have been prejudiced against her fiancé if she'd claimed Kelly was a hero ten times over. But *easy to be with?* What kind of a definition for a relationship was that?

Emma immediately stood, too, as if realizing how long they'd been talking. "I'll help you take this all in if you'd like. But then I'd better be getting back to the gallery—"

He snagged her wrist. Just lightly. Just to see what touching her did—to her, to him. All he actually did was wrap his fingers around her wrist, his thumb on her pulse, for a few bare seconds. Yet that instantly her eyes shot to his like a light beam. The pulse caught in her throat where he could see it, beating, beating. Her lips suddenly parted.

"He sounds like a saint, Emma," Garrett said.

"Not a saint. But a really good man—"

"Yeah. So you keep saying. And I believe you. But if you don't love him, why are you marrying him?"

She didn't answer him. Maybe she couldn't answer him. That close, she looked at his mouth, at his eyes. She didn't move away or try to evade his touch. A mourning dove called from somewhere in the yard.

The scent of peonies again drifted up on the hot, humid breeze, so teasing, so evocative.

It was all he could do not to kiss her—partly because that's how she looked at him, as if it were all she could do not to kiss him.

Facts kept flashing in his mind: that she was engaged, that he wasn't a poacher. But even when they were kids he'd never felt a tug this strong. At the vast age of thirty-five, it seemed crazy to discover there was a huge need inside him, a need from the heart, an unbearable hole of loneliness that he hadn't even known he was suffering from, a hole that only she could feel or fill.

"Don't, Garrett," she whispered softly, a plea.

He heard the tremor in her voice. Immediately he released her wrist and stepped back. "I didn't scare you, did I? I wouldn't hurt you for the world, Emma—"

"I never thought you would."

"But I won't lie. I do want you."

"Damn, you were always hopelessly honest. But didn't anyone ever tell you that you don't have to be quite this blunt?"

She obviously wanted him to smile, wanted to say something that would ease the tension between them. Just then, though, he couldn't seem to conjure up a smile, even for her. Instead he touched her cheek with the back of his hand, just the mildest—nakedest—of caresses. "Maybe you don't feel the same thing I'm feeling."

She sucked in a breath. "I feel it."

"Do you feel it with him, too, then? When you're making love with him?" He really had tried to drill some of the blunt honesty from his character, and God knows he didn't want to make Emma uncomfortable. But he had to ask. He just couldn't imagine loving someone and feeling this for someone else. Sure, you could be attracted to more than one person. But this yank on his heart as if he'd die if he couldn't have her, no. He couldn't imagine another woman in his life if he could have what he was feeling right now for Emma.

She shifted her gaze away from his. "I don't exactly know, Garrett. Reed and I haven't…gotten that close."

"Pardon?" He must have misheard her. She and Reed were engaged. How could they not have slept together?

She sighed heavily and noisily, glanced up at the sky as if begging for strength and then aimed straight for the stairs. As if they'd been discussing the weather, she said cheerfully, "If I find more goodies in the gallery I can spare, I'll bring them over. And if anything I brought is in your way or you don't like it, just give a shout and I'll come get it."

He leaned over the railing, watching her slim fanny swish as she climbed down the stairs. "Does that mean you're not too annoyed with me for asking a few awkward questions?"

"Of course I'm annoyed. You're being a royal pain. Unsettling and upsetting." She glanced back at him one more time. "No different than you always were. But thank God I'm not seventeen anymore."

"Damn straight. You're a hell of a lot more beautiful. And more confounding."

"And you always did like putting your hand in the fire. But we're going to get along famously while you're in town," she informed him cheerfully. "Partly because we're two doors down from each other. and because I care about your sister and want to help with Caroline if I can. And partly because you were my first love, which I really don't want to forget—even though you're being bad. Bad to the bone. Bad all the way down to the—"

"I get the picture."

"So the point is that I'm not going to let a little awkwardness make it impossible to be together now and then."

"Be together…how exactly do you mean that?"

She flipped him the finger. Emma. Emma Dearborn. Emma D—the silk-and-pearls debutante of Eastwick, the never-do-anything-wrong-in-public, never-offend-anyone Emma. Flipped him the finger.

He was downright charmed. And captivated.

"Damn, you're fun," he said.

"I am not."

He chuckled. "Yeah, you are. And I may just have to make another pass at you, Em."

"You try it and I'll have to slap you silly," she warned him…and then seemed to realize she was calling out that information to the entire neighborhood. He heard her sigh. Again. And then finally she disappeared from his sight.

He hung over the porch rail after that for a while, though. He could feel the silly grin on his face, when, hell, he didn't do grins. Come to think of it, he hadn't smiled in a long time.

He waited for the guilt to hit him again. And of course,

it did. It wasn't comfortable or right, this huge, building thing he felt for a woman who was taken, even though she sounded less taken than he'd originally believed.

Garrett told himself to back off. But when he pivoted around and headed into his apartment, he couldn't swear that he was going to obey that inner conscience.

He couldn't swear to anything. Not where Emma was concerned.

Except that he wished he hadn't been crazy enough to lose her the first time.

Emma twisted and turned until she could see the middle of her back in the bathroom mirror at Color. There it was. The reason for the itch that had been driving her crazy on and off for days now.

A brand new hive.

Just one, but now she had a fresh excuse for being a nervous wreck. Sure, that last conversation with Garrett had preyed on her mind like a cat on a mouse. She'd been making love with Garrett in her dreams. She'd been driving in traffic and suddenly feeling herself flush when thoughts of him swam to the surface. She'd been dressing in the morning, picking out slips of satin and lace and suddenly thinking of taking them off. For Garrett. With Garrett.

But now at least she could claim a physical reason for feeling as if she'd lost control of her life. Impatiently she scratched the sucker-hive on her back, washed her hands and hiked down the hall. The country club June dance was coming up tomorrow. She'd been thinking of it as D-night. Reed had had his hands full all week. Tomorrow she simply had to find a way to corner him alone, to say the things she'd failed to the last time.

And right now what she needed was work. Mind-numbing plain old hard work.

In one of the first-floor display rooms, Emma was finishing up an exhibit. Through July, she was calling it the Red Room. She'd combined textures and textiles with only the color in common. A headdress from Cameroon was juxtaposed with a marble sculpture of a young woman covered in rose petals. A Schweitzer linen wall hanging contrasted with an Afghani rug. A perfectly ghastly lamp from the 1950s—with a woman's leg in fishnet stockings for a base—echoed the shock and sensuality of a globe painted with the glossy red paint used by Jaguar.

The wall hanging wasn't right, though, so she took it down and tried again. No matter how hard she concentrated, a question kept staining the back of her mind. Exactly what did she owe Reed?

She stepped back and knew immediately she'd hung it too high.

How could she possibly make a major life decision based on feelings for a man who'd only been back in her life for a couple of weeks? And darn it, why did Garrett ever have to come back into her life? She'd known there were issues in her marriage with Reed. But she might have been able to make Reed happy—might have been able to settle herself—if Garrett had just never come home.

She stepped back from the linen wall hanging and gritted her teeth. Now she'd hung it too low.

"Hey, Emma." Josh poked his head in the doorway. He was working in the front with a group of volunteer kids—

they'd battled over who got to do that job because they both loved working with the teenagers, but Josh had won. This time. "Your mother's on the phone in the office."

"Thanks." Could this day get more frustrating? But it could, she discovered, when she picked up the phone in the office and heard her mother's slurred voice.

"Emma?"

"Mom. It's only three in the afternoon!"

"Couldn't help." Emma heard the *chink-chink* of ice cubes. "Your father…" The phone dropped or something else made a heavy thump. "…so mean. Nothing I do is right. Come home tonight? You have to. I need you."

After that cheery call, Emma returned to the wall-hanging project, thinking, okay, okay, what did she owe her parents? And how come she couldn't seem to escape any of the hairy life questions today, no matter how hard she tried?

To add insult to injury, she still hadn't conquered the wall-hanging problem before noticing a silver van with Weddings By Felicity for a logo. Seconds later a platinum blonde flew into the room, wearing heels too tall to walk on and a short, sassy haircut that matched her short, sassy print dress. "Oh, good, you're not busy!"

Emma glanced at the boxes heaped all over the room. "Felicity—"

Her old friend motioned with her head toward the door—since both her hands were filled, one with a long bottle of wine, the other with two crystal glasses. "You and I are going to talk. Right now. Don't even try arguing with me."

"I'm not arguing. I'm always glad to see you. But—"

"Uh-uh. No buts. Move the tush, cookie. We're drinking

and talking behind closed doors for at least the next half hour, and that's that."

Felicity looked a lot like a young Meg Ryan, except that Meg used to play such nice roles in movies, and Felicity shared more in personality with an army tank. She set up behind Emma's steamed-cherry desk, burrowed in her purse for a corkscrew and, predictably, found one. She poured one glass to the brim and shoved papers aside to push it toward Emma.

"If you weren't one of my dearest friends, I'd have mopped the floor with you long before this."

"Me?" The sign over Emma's desk said Our Lives Are Reflected in the Things We Choose. Ironic, she thought, because the gallery was brimful of elegance and style in all forms, yet her office walls were wallpapered with children's work. Finger painting. Shaving-cream art. Pictures made from macaroni and spangles and beads and buttons. Of course, no one ever hung out in the gallery office but her. And bossy, nosy, intrusive friends, it seemed.

"Look," Felicity said firmly. "I know that Reed's already made the honeymoon plans. Which means you both have to know when the wedding's going to be, yet somehow you still aren't calling me to pin down the date."

"I know. And I'm sorry. It's wrong…." She looked down at the wineglass. "Felicity, honestly, I can't drink in the middle of the day."

"Of course you can. Because we need to talk, and right now you're way too buttoned-up. Now listen to me." Felicity leveled herself into the wraparound red velvet chair and cocked her very long leg with its very tall heel on Emma's priceless desk. "I've been through this a million times. I know brides like no one knows brides. Brides get cold feet. It's nothing new, nothing to be ashamed of. In fact, you're likely to get colder feet than most."

"Why do you think that? That I'd get colder feet than most?"

"Because you're the kind to take marriage more seriously than the rest of us," Felicity said as if that should have been obvious. "Admit it. You think marriage is for keeps, don't you?"

"Well, yes."

"I rest my case. You're hopelessly naive. But that's not the point, Em. The point is that nerves like yours are why Weddings By Felicity exists. So I can take the stress off your back. And because this one's about you, and I love you, I don't care if it all has to be done at the last minute. I'll make it happen. It's also a lot easier to make it happen because it's at your mom's place. And when there's no limit on money, obviously that's a major help, as well." Felicity downed another sip of wine. "Although, I have to say, your mother is driving me batty. She wants everything her way."

Emma was listening. It was just… All right, she wasn't listening. She hadn't been listening to anyone or anything in days now. Ever since that afternoon with Garrett, she seemed to have suffered a complete brain meltdown. She just couldn't seem to stop replaying those moments. When he'd tugged her wrist and they'd been inches apart. When desire had risen in her like a fierce wildfire. She'd wanted to be kissed at that moment more than she'd wanted life or air. Wanted to kiss him. Wanted to be kissed by him. There'd been nothing else in her head, her heart, nothing. It was like being swooshed under by a tidal wave.

A tidal wave named Garrett.

And damn it, it was one thing to settle when you thought pale was all there was. But now she knew she hadn't come close to the possibilities before.

"Hey." Felicity snapped her fingers. "Wake up, you. Remember, I'm the one who paid for the great wine?"

"Yes. And that was really nice of you. And I'm sorry my mother's being a pain."

Felicity waved a hand. "Brides' moms and grooms' moms come with the territory. It's like having to eat your spinach when you're a kid. I can deal with it. And I can deal with your nerves, too, if you'll just let me. So either start talking to me or I'll have to slap you."

Emma understood she was supposed to laugh. But somehow what came out of her mouth was a question. "Do you think I'm a cold fish?"

"Huh? I was talking about cold feet, as in being nervous. Not cold fish, as in being frigid."

"But do you think I am? I mean…do I come across as less…sexual…than the rest of the group?"

"Oh, boy, this is getting good." Felicity dipped the wine bottle into her glass again, then squirmed her fanny back in the chair. "Honey, no one we grew up with is likely to wear a white dress at her wedding, if you know what I mean. Although…" She suddenly squinted at Emma. "Holy horseradish. You couldn't still be a virgin, could you? I didn't think it was possible."

"At my age? Come on," Emma scoffed and for the first time reached for her wineglass and took a gulp.

"You *couldn't* be," Felicity repeated, but she was still squinting at her. Squinting hard.

"I'm not. I'm not."

"Well…" Finally Felicity let it go. "Let's go back to the original question. What was the cold-fish remark all about?"

Emma couldn't sit. She walked over to the window, rubbed her itchy back against the frame. "There are a lot of reasons…why I'm no longer sure I'm the right person for Reed," she said quietly.

"Okay. Since you bought up the cold-fish thing, I assume sex is the real issue we're not talking about, right? And if that's all you're worried about, chill." Felicity relaxed again, as if relieved to discover nothing important was the problem. "Come on, you know it's the same for everyone. Sex is always great in the beginning. Then the first lust fades like the bloom on the rose. Then the couple both have to work at it—and good lovers do just that, so they tend to end up just fine. You know how it goes."

"Yes, of course I do," Emma said and this time filled the wineglass herself, keeping her expression averted.

"My theory, though, is that if it isn't great in the beginning, then the relationship just isn't worth going for. I mean, a guy who's selfish from the get-go never improves. That's not about sex, it's about a character flaw, you know?" Felicity suddenly looked startled. "Reed isn't that kind of selfish, is he? I mean, I barely know him. But he seems like such—"

Josh suddenly rapped on the open door. He rarely interrupted when she had someone in the office—partly because he rarely needed to. He was more than capable of handling most problems himself, but this time he clomped in with a frown, dropped something in her hand and closed her fingers around it. "You gotta quit putting that in the bathroom. I'm scared it's going down the drain," he said and then clomped right back out of the room again.

Emma knew what it was without looking…but she did look. There, in her palm, was the breathtaking sapphire Reed had given her.

She just couldn't seem to keep the engagement ring on her finger lately. Couldn't even try to pretend.

Felicity didn't seem to notice the exchange, just kept on chatting. Eventually she stood up to leave—although not until the bottle was nearly leveled. She carried the two crystal glasses and the corkscrew as far as the doorway, but then stalled there, clearly in no hurry to leave…not once they started on everyone else's gossip.

"Did you hear the police talked to Abby again? Apparently she got them to take fingerprints of her mother's safe—and they found a thumb and forefinger—and the prints weren't of any family members! So they're questioning Edith Carter again. You know, Bunny's housekeeper—"

"I just don't get it," Emma said, closing her hands around the ring again, feeling the stone pinch. "When it comes down to it, Abby's mom only told a bunch of gossip. Sure, people wouldn't want it in print if they were discovered sleeping in the wrong bed. But to kill her?"

"I know, I know. But then if someone had the cojones to blackmail Jack Cartright, you have to believe some people get pretty shook up over their secrets being told."

"Yeah," Emma said thoughtfully, again feeling the weight and shape of the sapphire in her palm.

"And another secret thing…I ran into Mary Duvall again. I know you used to be good friends with her."

"Yeah, we were really close back in high school."

"I think she's great. But she just looks so different than when we were in school. Suddenly turned into a Pendleton-and-pearls type. No more wild cookie. I think there's another mystery there."

"Maybe she just grew up," Emma said drily.

"And maybe she has a deep, dark secret that made her want to come hide out at home again… Hey, I heard maybe they were going to let Caroline out of the hospital in another day or two. Maybe, anyway. You haven't heard what her secret is, have you?"

"No."

"Well, it has to be something big. A girl doesn't swallow a bucket of pills if she's got nothing going on behind locked doors. God, this town. Big money makes for big secrets, eh?"

When Felicity finally left, Emma set the engagement ring on her desk and let out a sigh softer than a southern wind. Her family had secrets, too. But right now her own private heartache of a secret weighed so heavily on her conscience that she could barely think.

There was going to be hell to pay if she ducked out of a marriage this far along in the planning stages. But the more she worried about what she owed Reed—and what she owed her parents—the more she slowly realized that in her entire life she'd never asked the buffalo side of that nickel question.

Wasn't there some point in a woman's life when she got to ask, what did she owe herself?

Six

Garrett hurried through the hospital doors, past desks, past people, past carts, past anything and everything. Because the elevator was too slow, he took the stairs. He stumbled on the top step. Hell, a man could hardly run in the slick-soled dress shoes he was stuck wearing with a tux.

His tie still wasn't tied—he never could do tux ties. But he'd been dressed and grabbing the car keys to drive to the Eastwick Country Club dance when he got the call from the hospital.

At the head nurse's desk he barked, "Where is she?"

His sister's room had been changed. She wasn't back in Critical Care, thank God, but they'd moved her to the small psychiatric unit, where they could keep her monitored full-time. Caroline's recovery had seemed on a clear upswing until an event that afternoon, when the doctor feared she was a suicide risk again.

Just outside her room he slowed his step so he didn't barrel in there like a noisy elephant. But his stomach tightened when he saw his sister. She was lying on the bed, all curled up like a wounded baby, facing the wall. Straps on her wrists prevented her from removing the IVs or getting up on her own.

The same thought kept echoing in his mind—that he wished Emma were with him. She'd know what to say, what to do. He knew how to work, how to make money but not how to deal with people. He never had.

His sister must have sensed his presence, because she suddenly turned her head. "Hey, big brother," she murmured.

"Hey back."

She noticed his tux. "Whew. You're looking so hot that I want to whistle, but my throat seems to be mighty dry. They gave me something awfully strong." She wasn't completely lucid. Her eyes kept sluggishly opening and closing. "You all dressed up to take me out for a night on the town?"

"I'd take you out in two seconds if you'd go." He yanked a chair closer, parked on it. "Who phoned you, Caro?"

"What do you mean?"

"You know exactly what I mean. You were doing fine. We all thought you were coming home in another day or so. Then the nurse said you got a call this afternoon—"

"That day nurse is such a tattletale."

Garrett ignored that. "And the next thing, she found you in the bathroom with a piece of broken glass in your hand."

"It was an accident. I broke the water glass—"

"Quit it, Caro. It wasn't an accident. Who called you?"

he repeated, and when she didn't answer he said, "I know it was a local call, so it <u>had</u> to be someone from Eastwick. What in God's name is going on that's got you so terrorized? Tell me."

She smiled. "Aw, Garrett, you were always my white knight. You always got between me and Dad when I was in trouble. Or between me and a wrong date." She closed her eyes. "Do you remember when I had a sleepover that one time? Think we were all twelve. Raided the liquor cabinet after Mom and Dad went to bed, all got drunk as skunks, then decided to go swimming. Then you showed up, remember?"

"I remember. All six girls hurled all over me, as I recall. Not counting the messes all over the house."

"But you saved us all, Garrett." She smiled at him again. "You've got everybody fooled that you're a coldhearted workaholic. Through thick and thin, I could always count on you. You're the only one in the whole family with integrity. Real integrity."

"Obviously they're giving you some kind of hallucinatory drug. And all this being nice isn't getting you off the hook. It's time you told me what's going on."

"What's going on," she said thickly, slowly, "is that I made a mistake I can't live with."

Again he wished desperately that Emma was here. Emma wasn't judgmental and she had a way of calming people down, making them believe things would be all right. Instead his sister was stuck with just him. "There's no mistake you can't live with, Caroline. Nothing I couldn't forgive you for. Nothing I wouldn't help you get through. But I can't prove that to you if you won't talk to me."

"You want to help? Then get the hospital to release me so I can go home," she said.

Yeah, sure. And have her get another call at home from the person who'd been terrorizing her? Hell, he didn't know what to do. But when his sister fell asleep, he stumbled out of the hospital and aimed straight for the country club.

He wasn't remotely in a party mood, but this summer shindig was one of the year's biggest galas. Someone there knew what was going on with Caroline. They had to. And Emma might have some ideas about who to question that he hadn't thought of.

From a half mile away he started seeing the lights. The place was lit up like a miniature galaxy. The multiple French doors of the formal ballroom gaped open onto the patio. People were dancing both inside and out. Fountains sparkled with rainbow-hued water. Formally attired waiters carried sterling trays. The guys were all in tuxes, but the women wore every color in the universe—bridal whites and sassy reds, sea-greens and shimmery yellows, the glitter nearly blinding even from the distance where he parked. Jewels twinkled and shimmered on every neck, every ear, every wrist.

Garrett walked around to the back entrance, away from the crush, hoping to slip into the crowd without being noticed. In the old days, the club would have hired an orchestra. These days, club members tolerated a traditional waltz now and then, but they also wanted spice for their money—rock and roll, fandangos, music with a beat and some sex to it. Still, some traditions never changed. Flowers spilled over onto wrists, in women's hair, scenting the centers of the tables.

He suddenly hesitated. He wasn't afraid of such gatherings.

He'd grown up in this echelon of Eastwick society. He'd rather be working than stuck making small talk, but that wasn't what suddenly made him pause.

From a distance, the scene looked like a dream, with beautiful people laughing, dancing, enjoying each other. That was what it had always been about, Garrett suddenly realized. Belonging. People didn't hunger to join the country club for the prestige of it.

They hungered to belong. To something. To someone.

When push came to shove, he figured that had to be the core of his sister's problem. He didn't know the how, the when, why or who. But the only threat worth the kind of despair Caroline was enduring had to emanate from that kind of source—the threat of losing someone who mattered.

Or maybe he was imposing his own hunger to belong on his sis's situation, he thought wryly. Until coming back home—until meeting up with Emma again—he'd never thought of himself as lonely. He'd never thought he needed anyone. Yet now that desire to be with her, to belong with her, was as fierce as—

And then he saw her. Emma was weaving through the dancers, then past them and outside, past the spill of lights and music on the patio. She'd surely have seen him—he was just standing in the tree shadows by the walk—if she hadn't been so obviously intent. She headed straight for the black iron gates of the club pool.

The pool was closed for swimming tonight, but the underwater lights had been left on for atmosphere. He watched Emma unlatch the gate, step inside and out of sight of the partyers. Her gown looked luminescent in the aquamarine light. The style made him think of a Roman toga, nothing fancy, just a swath of sapphire-blue fabric that draped over one shoulder and fell to her ankles. Slim gold ropes twisted around her waist and under the bodice.

The simplicity and classiness of the gown suited her perfectly.

She liked her jewels—what woman didn't?—yet she was wearing none tonight, unlike all the other women there. Her bare throat gleamed, her skin its own adornment. Her eyes had more shine and emotion than any gem. His heart surged just to see her, just for the chance of being near her.

But she wasn't alone.

She was talking to the one man Garrett kept conveniently trying to forget. Her fiancé. And it looked as if they were having a damn serious private talk, because Reed Kelly had the posture of a man who was furious enough to snap.

Emma thought she'd go out of her mind. Naturally she couldn't talk seriously to Reed in the middle of the club dance, but she had hoped they could take off halfway through the evening, and then she'd have a chance to talk with him privately.

That was her goal, but she just couldn't seem to make it happen. She'd barely seen Reed for two seconds since they'd arrived, much less had a prayer of escaping. Being in charge of the club's fund-raising committee didn't help, because everyone and his mother stopped to chat.

The social craziness started when frail, slender Frank Forrester cornered her. Frank had been so generous to the club and community that she couldn't avoid speaking with him. Besides, he was a darling—although Delia, his current wife, was quite an experience. Lots of women visited a plastic surgeon for one reason or another, but Delia's boobs were so fake they looked like mighty ball bearings. She'd gone for a tight sheath in a glitzy lamé and covered every finger in rings. To each his own, Emma always thought, but Delia was so, so unlike the quietly generous Frank.

After that, Emma had to spend a few minutes with the Debs Club—all the girls were there, with either their mates or appropriate rail meat. Felicity, of course, kept shooting her meaningful looks, as if determined to remind her of their earlier conversation. And then Mary Duvall showed up, covered modestly from her throat to her ankles, very quietly making her way through the crowd, looking as if she needed a friend and someone to reintroduce her to Eastwick again, so obviously Emma had to step in there.

Abby Talbot swung her away from Mary for a while after that. Gossip was still buzzing about her mother's death—and who was going to take on writing the *Eastwick Social Diary*. It was the gossip and mudslinging everyone missed most. Abby was using the dance as a means to ask questions. She looked gorgeous, as always, but her mother's death seemed to have changed her from a quiet, gently understanding kind of woman into a steamroller. She wanted answers.

And if she wanted justice, she had lost all faith she was going to get it through the police investigation.

After that, Emma was corralled by Jack and Lily Cartright. Emma had gotten involved in the Eastwick Cares organization—where Lily had been a social worker—several years before, so they'd become friends. Heaven knew

Emma loved working with the teenagers. This time, though, Lily tracked her down, looking radiant and blooming, to ask if she had any free time the following week for a special kids' project.

Emma said yes. Darn it, her schedule was too packed to add any more to it, but she'd never been good at saying no to anything involving kids, and by then she'd been too frazzled to even try.

Reed found her and swirled her into a waltz, but almost immediately they were separated again. Someone claimed Reed's attention at the same time Garrett's parents descended on her. Barbara and Merritt Keating were using every public opportunity to say that their daughter, Caroline, was all right. She'd just accidentally taken "the wrong pill" and had "a chemical reaction."

"You know so many people in Eastwick, Emma," Barbara said. "It would help so much if you'd help set the record straight."

"Garrett's around here somewhere," his father boomed. "He'll tell everyone, too. We're very concerned about some of the hurtful rumors we've heard spread about Caroline."

Immediately Emma searched the crowd for Garrett yet couldn't spot him. Her mother grabbed her arm before she had another chance to even try. Her mom was dressed in ivory—her favorite color—and looked slim and elegant. Only the slightest slur in her speech would give anyone the impression that she'd started partying much earlier that day. Her drinking was one of the best-kept secrets in Eastwick, but tonight her mom was on a happy buzz for a different reason.

"I heard from Felicity that you were likely going to

announce the wedding date for sure. Like tonight, dear? I admit, I've been passing a little hint around our friends…."

Emma's pulse picked up a frantic beat. She'd meant to talk to Reed tonight—but now she knew she had to talk to him immediately, before her mother started spreading the wedding gossip even further. All these dutiful conversations had been necessary, and truthfully she loved all these people, had all her life. But now she had to find Reed and drag him to a private spot somewhere, somehow.

She found him talking to a wannabe senator and snagged his wrist. He was happy to be dragged off, but not for the reasons she had in mind. Long before she'd gotten them out to the private spot by the pool, she'd known this talk was going to be hard. But she started out saying honestly, "Reed, I'm not sure either of us really wants this marriage," and he just didn't seem to believe her.

He went back to fetch her a drink, a pinot noir—her favorite—and then walked around the pool to a spot where they were completely cut off from any view of the partyers. He seemed determined to believe she had bridal nerves or that she was fussing over the stress of putting on the wedding.

Finally, though, he seemed to pick up that the tears in her eyes weren't from a minor case of stress. "All right, Emma. Just say it straight. What is all this really about?"

She desperately wanted that wine to soothe her nerves, yet she put it down, afraid she'd choke on it. She'd never deliberately, willingly, hurt anyone. "Reed, you don't really want me. You have to know it."

"Huh? Of course I want you. Why on earth would I

have asked you to be my wife if I didn't want you to be part of my life?"

She pressed her hand to her stomach. "I mean sex, Reed. You don't feel any big attraction for me."

Reed never lost his temper. He had more patience than Job. But she could see he was stretching to keep it together by then. "You're the one who didn't want to sleep together until we were married."

"I know."

"You felt strongly about it. As you put it, people sleep together like it's automatically on their to do list after they've been together a while, rather than it being something unique or special for the two of them. That's why you wanted to do it the old-fashioned way—waiting. Because you wanted intimacy to be something more."

"I know I said that. And I meant it."

"You said you were tired of casual values. And so am I. As far as I know, we weren't waiting because of not *wanting* each other."

"But you don't," she said quietly. "Want me."

"Of course I do. For Pete's sake, Emma. This is a ridiculous conversation. You're a gorgeous woman. You can't possibly believe that desire wasn't part of the equation."

She persisted. "If you wanted me—the right way, the way I'd like to be wanted—you wouldn't have waited. And it's the same for me. I love you. You're a wonderful, wonderful man. And for a long time I believed that kind of love would make a good marriage—"

"But now you suddenly don't," he said with exasperation.

She nodded. "I think we'd…manage. But in the long run, I think we'd both be miserable. Lonely. That we would never have the kind of marriage your parents have, but more my parents' kind of arrangement, because the chemistry just isn't there."

He fell silent, looking at her, clearly considering what she said. "I could argue with you, keep trying to talk. But I can see your mind's made up. You want to call it off," he said.

She pulled the sapphire off her finger, offered it to him. When he didn't take it, she gently tucked it in his chest pocket. But he still wouldn't look at it.

"I'll tell everyone it's my fault. Because it is," she said.

He immediately dismissed that idea. "You're going to get a ton more backlash out of this than I will. I'll take the blame. But right now..." He shook his head, then spun around. "Right now I think I'll just take off. Disappear for a few days. If you don't mind, I really don't want to talk to you for a while."

He walked away from her, past the pool gate, yanking off his tux jacket as he headed straight for his car.

Emma couldn't remember the last time she felt lower than a skunk.

She'd never have chosen to hurt as good a friend, as good a man, as Reed.

Yet no matter how badly she felt about hurting him, deep in her heart she felt the steady beat of relief. For the first time in months she felt as if she could breathe.

Tomorrow there'd undoubtedly be gossip hell to pay when Eastwick caught wind of the broken engagement. But for right now she was free—and that included the freedom to be as upset as she needed to be. She whirled around, thinking that she needed to return to the ballroom to retrieve her bag and wrap before she could get out of there. For just an instant she thought she glimpsed the shadow of movement in the shady trees beyond the wrought iron gate. Someone there?

Whether there was or there wasn't, she headed back into the ballroom. She seemed to be shaking from the tension of the whole emotional scene. She wanted to go home—or back to the gallery—as quickly as she could get her things. Escape was the only thing on her mind.

At four-thirty in the morning, Emma had given up pretending she could sleep. Sipping a cup of tea, she sat on the screened back porch at the gallery, still dressed in her evening gown but barefoot now, and when the evening temperature had dipped, she'd scared up an old sweater from the shop to drape over her shoulders.

She had to look pretty ridiculous, but there was no one around to see. The sun wasn't due up for at least another hour. And although lack of sleep was undoubtedly going to catch up with her, she was trying to bolster some peace into her system before facing the day ahead. She knew it wasn't going to be easy.

Before leaving the country club, she'd cornered her mother to let her know the engagement was off—it was the only way to stop her mom from talking up the wedding for the rest of the evening. By the time Emma arrived back at the gallery, though, her phone had rung nonstop.

Her mother had called several times. Then Felicity and other friends.

Then her father.

Even between phone calls, she'd thrown up, which struck her as darn near funny. Everyone in Eastwick always thought of her as calm, cool and collected. She was the diplomat of the Debs, not the instigator—the peacemaker, never the confronter. And this, of course, was why. Whenever she had to do confrontations, she heaved.

Her stomach had settled down hours before, and she'd turned off her cell phone and all the landlines inside Color. It was so late the crickets and frogs had stopped chirping. So late the baby moon had started dipping low in the sky. So late there hadn't been the sound of a car passing in hours.

Still, she leaned her head back against the rough porch wall and couldn't seem to find an ounce of peace.

In the darkness she heard the backyard gate latch, saw a tall, dark shadow—and probably should have responded with fear. Yet she didn't.

By the time Garrett climbed the step and rapped softly on the screen door, she already knew it was him.

Unlike her, he was dressed in comfortable old chinos and a shirt, the kind of clothes someone intelligent would wear at this time of the morning. But at the moment she didn't feel intelligent. She felt vulnerable and shaken. Too vulnerable to want to see a man who'd come to mean way, way too much to her.

"I told myself to leave you alone, but I saw the light in the gallery when I first got home. I never saw it turned off. Started worrying that you were still up, even this late. And I can see you are." He stepped in, quickly closed the screen against mosquitoes. But instead of approaching her, he went to the far side of the screened porch and hunkered down on the Japanese mat. "See me? I'm staying on the other side of the porch. Not causing any trouble. Not planning to. But…I saw you. With your fiancé. At the pool."

"I thought someone was there." Her pulse started that dancing thing again, just from being with him. "There was no reason for you to worry about me, Garrett."

"Worry is what I do. What good would it be to be a hard-case obsessive workaholic if I didn't know how to worry constantly? And it kept bugging me… You had to have had a mighty rough night."

"Yeah, well…I think a woman's supposed to have a miserable night when she's been a creep."

"After you left, the gossip swooped over the club like a tidal wave. The talk was that the marriage was off. But no one had a clue who called off the engagement. Or why. You two were supposed to be the perfect couple."

"The one who called it off—that'd be me. The creep in the story."

"Feeling pretty low, are you?"

"It hurts like the devil. I hate hurting people. I hate hurting someone who's been nothing but good to me even more. The whole thing…"

"Sucks?"

"A perfect word for it," she agreed miserably.

"Anything you want to vent?"

She didn't. Not to anyone. And maybe not to Garrett especially. Yet the silence had been beating inside her for hours now. Silence that wasn't as simple as guilt. "Reed's been a good friend for years. So I didn't just lose a fiancé. I lost a friend."

Garrett said nothing. Just leaned his head against the far porch wall the way she leaned her head in the shadows at her end.

"For a long time…for years…I was determined not to

marry, didn't want anything to do with marriage. I remember all that wild, lusty heat I felt with you…."

"So do I."

"But when you went off to college, broke it off, you know what? Once I was through suffering from a crushed heart, I started feeling relieved. Even as a girl, even that young, I was afraid of that chemistry." He didn't prod her, didn't push—which, damn him, made it all that much easier to spill her guts. "My parents have possibly one of the sickest marriages around. Not *the* sickest. But one of the true terrible-for-each-other relationships."

"My parents' marriage might be able to compete at that level."

"That's the thing. The money in this community, the power, is fabulous. There's so much potential to do so much good. And we do. I love this area. But when money and sex get together…" She shook her head expressively.

"I'm not sure I get it…how that relates to why you never wanted to marry."

"Because that's always how it is. Marriages here are mergers. A woman antes up on her side of the deal with sex, using her sexual skills to attract and keep the most powerful man. And I just…"

"What?"

"I just never wanted to live my life that way."

"Come on, Em. There was never any rule you had to play life by those conditions."

"A rule, no. But the pressure never let up. My parents, my grandmother, ardently wanted me to be married—to the right man, in the right family—to start having kids and adding to the Dearborn dynasty. And it seemed like Reed was an answer because he was such a good friend. Until you came home."

"Hey, how'd I enter this equation?"

"Because, you horrible man, I'd talked myself into believing for years that chemistry wasn't important. Didn't have to be important. I wasn't remotely afraid of a sexual relationship with Reed or worried it wouldn't be all right. I didn't want more. It never occurred to me that I was cheating *him* of more."

She leaned forward, shooting Garrett a harsh, stern glare in the darkness—even if she couldn't quite see his face.

"But you kissed me," she said softly. "And I was back remembering what it was like to be seventeen again. Hot and hungry. Full of yearning. And suddenly it wasn't enough to spend a whole lifetime of all right."

"I've been held responsible for a fair number of things in my lifetime. Being cold-blooded in business deals. Being clueless in relationships. Being tough in negotiations. But I don't think anyone ever suggested my kissing technique had any power before."

"You're joking. I'm not. Darn it, Garrett, you've ruined my life," she said. And stood.

Seven

Garrett saw her walking toward him in the dark shadows of the porch. He assumed she was coming close to engage in a more serious conversation. She'd just claimed that he'd ruined her life. Only there was something odd in her tone, not just the hint of humor he wasn't expecting, but something else.

That something else was in the gleam of her eyes when she leaned down…crouched down…and then pounced.

The aim on her first kiss missed the mark. Her lips smooshed his cheek, but then homed more accurately than radar on the target she really wanted. In the dark corner of the porch, where he was sitting cross-legged on a mat, he felt her elbow dig into his rib and her fanny nestle into his lap—initially threatening the family jewels. He caught a pale hint of perfume. Felt the silky long gown drift around him. Tasted the naked softness of her lips.

Unless he did something—and quickly—he suspected she was either going to injure or permanently maim him. Enthusiasm could be a dangerous thing, yet severing the kiss didn't seem to be an option.

In a thousand years he'd never expected Emma to jump him. She wasn't the jumping type. Yet more evocative than being jumped by Emma was her lack of finesse. She really couldn't have done this much. If ever.

And her lack of experience seemed to make his blood rush like a hot, wild river. Still latched onto her, he used one hand to snug down her spine, to lean her down, down, until she was lying on the mat. He still had a leg hooked under her, a knee threatening to break, but he managed to pull that loose and then he could lie with her. Length to length. Still latched together. And with both hands free now to hold her still, to frame her face, to invest pressure and emotion and promise into the next set of kisses.

He took her tongue. Heard her heave a sigh, a breathy, artless groan. A miserable groan of longing and wanting.

Her gown was held up by a swath of silk on one shoulder. That was all. Her other shoulder was bare, softer than a baby's butt, and when his lips trailed down, he found the soft thudding pulse in her throat, the fragile line of her collarbone. And that naked shoulder had him so damned mesmerized that he had to taste and nuzzle.

Her knee shot up as if she wanted to wind a leg around him, yet nearly connected with his family jewels again.

Control slipped. Garrett never let control slip. Not in life, not in work, not in sex. But hell, she was just so wild. For him. As impossible as it seemed, she was wild for him.

His emotional timbers were already shaken, he knew

that. He'd been up all night. No rest, no sleep. It bothered him fiercely that he'd seen that private scene between her and Reed. It bothered him that Reed hadn't fought for her the way a man should have fought for an unforgettable woman like Emma. It bothered him that she'd looked so bowed and cowed after Kelly left her.

For hours he'd told himself to stay out of it; her relationship with Reed was none of his business. Besides which, he was afraid it would embarrass Emma if he said anything. No one wanted scenes like that witnessed by anyone. Who was ever happy with how they broke up or fought with someone? Those scenes were always horrible.

But damn, it was so obvious that she'd felt terrible. And when he'd finally escaped the dance and hightailed it home, he'd found himself standing in his upstairs window, watching for lights at Color. Hell, he didn't even know if that's where she'd land that night. But then he'd seen the lights go on, a trail from the front of the gallery leading toward the back…and then nothing.

He'd paced. And paced. Naturally there wasn't much he could see from the second-story window two houses down from hers. When he'd gotten around to realizing that he was downright spying on her, he'd wanted to whack himself upside the head. He didn't do things like that. But finally he just couldn't stand it. He had to know she was all right.

And now he knew.

She wasn't all right.

Clearly she wasn't remotely all right.

She twisted from beneath him, knelt and tugged folds on folds up of the silky gown over her head. Beneath, she wore a satin thong. Her hair came down in a cloud around her cheeks, and before his brain had time to register how dazzling she was, how exquisite, she'd come back to him.

"Love me, Gar," she whispered. "We missed this last time around. I don't want to miss it again. I want to know— I've needed to know, all this time. What we are together. What we could have been."

Her voice, so like velvet, caressed him almost as evocatively as her hands. He dredged up some sanity from God knew where. "Emma, I didn't come here for this. I swear. I understand, you're upset—"

"Didn't you wonder how it would be between us?" she whispered.

"Yes." No way to deny it. No way to deny anything with her fingers, pleated open, skimming up, his ribs, his chest, to his neck…her lips only a breath away.

"I regretted it a million times. That we didn't make love back then."

"Me, too."

"I'm tired of regrets, Gar. I've lived by the rules every which way I know how. They're not working. I want you. I've wanted you forever. Are you going to say no?"

As if he could. Maybe a while back—a few minutes back—he might have still had a brain and some principles, but now any thinking power he'd ever had was pressing thick and hard against her belly. He'd label it lust, except this was a helluva lot more lethal than lust.

When he took her mouth this time, it was different. When he leveled her onto the mat, everything was different. He told himself that he'd turned into the seducer, yet it wasn't true. They were both on fire, both in a frenzy— to touch everywhere, to cherish, to claim.

He had no idea what happened to that satin thong, but there was nothing between them when it mattered. When he thrust inside her, he felt as if something shattered inside him, as if some part of him had been protected by a shell all his life, and with her that protective shell was lost.

He wanted her. Needed her. Like air, like fire, like earth. Her scent, her sounds, her taste…he wanted all of her, every which way from Sunday, now, immediately, completely.

She called his name, gripping him tightly with her inner muscles, inciting him higher, faster, harder. "Love me," she kept whispering softly, fiercely, as if there were ever a time when he hadn't.

When the first spasm of release shuddered through her, he could no longer hold back. Violent with need, relentless at driving her higher than she'd ever been, he rode them both to the edge…and then tipped over.

By the time he sank against her, burying his face in her hair, he couldn't have roused for a fire.

Nothing could have made him leave her.

Garrett had no idea how long he'd been asleep, but when his eyes suddenly opened, the sun was poking its head over the horizon. A soft, smoky light seeped through the porch screens. Robins were having an orgy in the dew-drenched grass, plucking worms. Someone's cat prowled the white picket fence line. And he was stroking Emma's back while she was stroking his. Side by side, both of their heads on the same jacquard pillow.

The mat beneath them was as comfortable and yielding as bamboo spikes. Still, he didn't move. He had the craziest feeling that he'd been looking into her eyes just like this, exactly like this, right before he'd completely crashed.

"Am I the only one who slept?" he murmured.

"No. I dropped off like a stone. Better than I've slept in weeks and weeks."

"But short." One of them must have pulled her Grecian gown over them. The morning was warm enough, yet the gown hardly made an adequate blanket. And still neither moved. "What time do you open the gallery?"

"Not until ten. But Josh'll be here by nine-thirty, latest."

"So we need all traces of crime erased by then?"

"The only crime I can think of," she murmured, "is that I never tried seducing you back when we were teenagers."

"You were pretty straight back then."

"Still am," she confessed.

"Not with me."

"Not with you," she whispered and kissed him. They couldn't have caught more than a couple hours' sleep, yet he was suddenly aroused again.

More than aroused. On fire. For her, only for her.

She closed her eyes and just seemed to lose herself in him. She responded blindly, fiercely, to every touch, every kiss, every sound, as if no man had ever seeped through her defenses the way he did, as if she'd never wanted before, never needed before.

Or maybe that was just him. Feeling that way about her. Even as a teenager, he couldn't recall feeling this crazy. He wanted to be with her more than he wanted life or breath. He didn't care about tomorrow. Didn't care about anything but having her, taking her and being taken.

As he tugged her beneath him, he hadn't forgotten his

sister's grave problems…or the public complications of Emma's called-off engagement. In a matter of hours, they both had to face the reality of heavy problems in their lives.

Maybe that propelled him to be a better lover than he was. A better lover than he thought he could be. But when Emma's legs were wrapped around him, her throat arched as she surrendered to release, he felt a wild, crazy rush that was far more than orgasmic.

All these years, he'd never married. In that instant he knew it was because he'd never really trusted anyone. In his world, he only trusted himself…. Yet he'd already trusted Emma with his fears about his sister, about his life. And now, irrevocably, he was trusting her with his heart.

With her, all his secrets were coming out of the woodwork.

He was in love with her.

Realizing it was the most terrifying sensation he could remember. But damn, it was beyond wonderful.

Emma left him sleeping, knowing how little rest he'd had. She took a few seconds to restore the gallery to order, turning off lights and turning on the phones, before hustling into the shower.

As she should have expected, the phone started ringing the instant she stepped under the spray. Her hair was foamed up with shampoo when she heard a second round of ringing. And she was drying off and tiptoeing around her bedroom off the porch when she heard it ring yet again.

Damn. Soon she had to start taking those calls. It didn't matter how exhausted she was, she knew she couldn't escape a full schedule today. She twisted her still damp hair into a chignon, pulled on a light linen skirt and T-shirt, pushed her feet into sandals, took a breath and then aimed back for the porch to find her lover.

It was in her heart, that beat. That find-her-lover beat. It wasn't familiar, the song, the music, yet in spite of everything—and God knows she knew she was facing Armageddon today—her heart couldn't seem to stop singing.

On the back porch she found Garrett, looking groggy-eyed and wild-haired, wearing undershorts…and making her want to laugh, because his cell phone looked glued to his ear. He couldn't escape his business life any more than she could escape hers.

For a moment she just savored the look of him. In high school, kids had pegged him as a brain more than a jock. But she'd gotten to know that bare chest back then, had always known his shoulders were like marble, his chest tightly muscled.

She hadn't known what a creative lover he'd be. And when he suddenly noticed her in the doorway, she realized she'd never known how vulnerable those wicked deep brown eyes could be, either. Emotion hung between them. Something warmer than the sultry morning, something magical. He lifted a hand in a gesture inviting her closer and immediately cut short the call.

"Hey, beauty," he murmured.

"Hey, you," she murmured right back. "I thought I heard your phone ringing several times, because your ringer sound is so different than mine. But I knew I was in for personal calls today. What's this for you—work calls start bugging you even before seven in the morning?"

"Hey, you don't get the plaque for being a workaholic if you get off the treadmill."

"But you get calls this early all the time?"

"Just the nature of the work, Emma." It was just idle conversation. He was looking at her. She was looking at him.

All she wanted was to climb back on that impossibly hard mat with him and make love all day. She'd never thought of herself as a fragile woman, but right now she felt more fragile than a single silk thread in the sunlight. It was Garrett's doing. When he'd found her last night, she'd been so, so low. Yet he'd made her feel like a woman, the way she'd never felt about herself as a woman.

She wanted to tell him. To show him.

But a long day was waiting for her. And she was unsure what last night had meant to him. Besides which, the circles under his eyes tattled how hard he'd been pushing it since he'd come home.

She shook her head. "Garrett, you were always that way. Driven. Committed. Never-say-die."

"I know. They're on the heavy lists of faults."

"They're wonderful qualities, you doofus. But for the next hour and a half you're turning off the phone and coming with me."

"Going where? And does the where have coffee?"·

"You're going finger painting. And yes, I'll get you coffee first."

"Finger painting. Yeah, right," he said with a laugh.

Naturally he thought she was joking. She bribed him—if he turned off his cell phone for an hour, she'd tell him the truth. By the time she'd successfully confiscated his phone, they were in her white van, carting mugs of almond-toffee java as she drove. And told.

It was one of her secrets. Not a big one, but nevertheless,

not public knowledge. Garrett knew Lily Cartright but not that Lily used to be a social worker for Eastwick Cares or that she'd hooked Emma up with the grief-counseling center.

"I still don't get it. How do you get from grief counseling to finger painting?"

She showed him. The building was new, built in a shady cul-de-sac with a water garden and ducks—although the ducks, she admitted, were strictly volunteer. When they walked inside, four children were sitting on candy-colored beanbags.

"Sheesh, you guys are early," she told the squirts, who swarmed them both. Martha was three, George was five, and the two four-year-olds were Elisabeth and Pops.

"Is *he* gonna paint with us, Ms. Dearborn?"

"I keeping telling you, you can call me just plain Emma, honest. And yes. His name is Garrett Keating. And believe it or not, he's never finger painted in his whole life." Because he looked stunned and scared at the door, she hooked his arm.

"You're kidding." Pops, the pint-size blonde with the twinkly-light tennies, took his other arm. "You're really old."

"Thanks," Garrett said.

"What'd you do when you were a kid? Like, if you never finger painted?" Elisabeth wanted to know.

"He probably doesn't remember. He's old," the pint-size blonde volunteered again.

Emma steered them past the open kitchen, past the central meeting place. The rooms were constructed in a wagon-wheel fashion.

Older teenagers were given a room with easy chairs and cuddling blankets. Preteens had a room with games and walls they could write on. The little ones, though, were hers.

Her room could be hosed down—or that equivalent. Good thing, because the art projects she got the squirts into invariably involved paint or clay or something that got on everything. Before handing out aprons—including one for Garrett that made her babies all laugh—she hid the phones from harm's way.

When she set her cell phone next to Garrett's on a safe top shelf, she noticed immediately that she'd missed a half-dozen calls since last night—three of them from her mother. She gulped. But not for long.

Later today she'd deal with her mother and all the other realities related to her broken engagement. This morning was about something else. The kids…and Garrett. Garrett, who made tons of money and took tons of responsibility. Garrett, who'd been so tender and passionate with her. Garrett, who never played.

There wasn't much she could give back to him, but she could darn well teach him to play. She just wanted these moments of magic to last as long as they could. For her. But for him, too.

"Now, stop looking at Mr. Garrett. He has to wear my apron because we don't have one his size. We don't laugh at other people, do we?"

"No," Garrett said pitifully and got the kids laughing again.

She gathered them around the table as she set out supplies. "Okay. I want everybody to close your eyes. I know you've all felt sad lately. But this morning I want you to concentrate. I want you to think about something happy. Something beautiful. And that's what I want you to paint. Colors that you think are beautiful. Colors that make you happy to look at."

"I don't know. Is he too old to be happy?" Pops cocked her head toward Garrett.

Emma intervened before Garrett needed to come up with an answer. "No one's ever too old to be happy. But sometimes things happen that make us sad. We can't make that feeling go away. But it can help if we remember what makes us happy. So…are you all ready to try?"

"I'd better help him." Again Pops cocked her head at Garrett with a sigh, as if the job were so weighty she was tired already.

A little more than an hour later, the last urchin had been picked up. Another age group was occupying rooms at the center when Emma and Garrett left the building. Emma had to tease him. "I've never seen a four-year-old flirt before. What a femme fatale."

"Flirt? *Flirt?* She was a four-year-old curmudgeon. Nothing I did was right. And she laid it on damn thick about my being old, old, old."

"She fell in love with you on sight. Couldn't you tell?"

"Was that before or after she finger painted a red heart on my sleeve?" He motioned to the eloquent red paint on his sleeve. "Does this come out?"

"It should. But if it doesn't, I'll bet you can afford another shirt."

Before they reached her van, she hooked his hand, then lifted up on tiptoe and framed his face with her palms. "I hate to tell you this…"

"Uh-oh. Nothing good ever follows 'I hate to tell you this'—"

"But you're smiling to beat the band. You're relaxed. You had a fabulous time with the kids," she said smugly.

"I'm not admitting anything. How could I possibly have had a good time finger painting with a bunch of hellions?"

"It beats me—but you were right in the thick of it all. I think you made a bigger mess than they did. That seems like headline news to me. In fact, if Bunny were still alive, I could call her, put it in the infamous *Eastwick Social Diary*. No one would believe this huge a scandal unless they saw it in print."

His eyes narrowed. But he hadn't moved, didn't seem to mind her pinning him with her hands. "You've got an evil side to you, Emma Dearborn."

"Oh, thank you. That's the nicest thing anyone's said to me in years and years."

She wasn't sure how it happened, but somehow she'd ended up in his arms again. In fact, he'd seemed to quite arrogantly lean against the shady side of her van and nestle her right into the V of his thighs. "You want to hear nice things?" he questioned.

She sobered, because he'd suddenly dropped the easy, teasing tone. Her eyes softened. "What I want…is for you not to regret last night."

"That's my line, Em. When you woke up this morning, I was afraid you'd think I took advantage of you."

"The way I remember it, I jumped you. So I should get the credit for taking advantage, not you."

But he wasn't buying that. And though he was holding her close, his gaze kindled more than desire. "You'd just been through a really emotional situation. You were upset, vulnerable. I came over because your lights stayed on so late…. I just got worried, thought you might need someone to talk to, vent on. But I swear, I wasn't trying to cause an awkward complication in your life."

She said quietly, honestly, "Garrett, you *are* a complication for me. You have been ever since you came home."

He went still. Wary-still. A car pulled into the center's parking lot. Noisy kids spilled out. He never noticed, never looked away.

She took a nervous breath. "I think a lot of people would judge my making love with you yesterday as wrong. Wrong because I was so recently engaged, wrong because it looked like a rebound thing. But I want you to know…it wasn't like that. What you've done since you came home was bring out feelings in me that I didn't know I had. All kinds of feelings. Not just sexual ones. If I'd married Reed, it would have been wrong. That's the truth."

"You sound very sure."

"I'm absolutely positive. I love Reed the way you love a wonderful close friend. But I never loved him…sexually. Intimately. To be totally honest, I thought the feelings I had for him were all there was. For ages I just thought I'm not a particularly sexual person—"

"You can't be serious."

She felt his thumb nudging a strand of hair on her cheek that had loosened from its chignon. His touch was so tender she wanted to shiver. "I'm very serious. It was always easy for me do the celibate thing. In principle, for darn sure, I never wanted to be courted because I was an heiress to the Dearborn money, didn't want to be part of some merger. But now, I realize that it was easy to hold tight to those principles…because I was never really tempted."

"The guys growing up here used to be so smart. They must have gotten a lot stupider in the years I was away."

She smiled because he wanted her to. "You're going to think this is mighty Pollyannaish, but…"

"But what?"

"But I wanted making love to be beautiful or I never wanted it at all. In the grand scheme of things, I realize beauty doesn't rate up there as seriously important. It's hardly world peace or curing world hunger or anything. But I always felt…beauty does matter. It can make a difference. Beauty around us can give us peace and hope and…" She started to laugh at herself… "And all that nonsense."

"That's not nonsense, Emma."

"Well, I realize it's hardly a realistic view of the world. Which, God knows, my family is always telling me. But I'm just trying to say that last night was beautiful. For me. It was what I'd held out for. And I'm glad I did."

She raised up again and kissed him. Not a kiss of enticement. Just…she wanted to give him something sweet and honest. So her lips brushed his, softer than a whisper. More fleeting than a promise.

She didn't know what he wanted from her. What he felt. There's no way she would have asked. It was crazy to think he could possibly care as fiercely and deeply as she did—not this soon. Not in this short a time. But her heart was filled to brimming over with emotions and choices and wonder that she hadn't expected to feel.

Right or wrong, crazy or not crazy—impossible or not impossible—she knew she'd fallen in love with him.

Eight

Late-afternoon sun poured through the windshield as Emma turned into her parents' driveway. As she shut off the engine and climbed out, she took a long, bracing breath.

This visit was going to be difficult, but it had to be done. She owed her parents a more extensive explanation about Reed and the broken engagement. And this afternoon was the best possible time to handle this, because she felt a rare surge of strength—not the poise she put on in public but darn near something real. She actually wanted to have this talk with her parents, wanted to be honest with them. It amazed her.

She knew Garrett was the catalyst for that boost of confidence. Darn it, at her age, she shouldn't need somebody else to validate her. But he had. He'd made her feel accepted and wanted for who she was—not who others wanted her to be. And as she hiked to the front door, she felt an easiness on the inside she hadn't experienced in a month of Sundays.

Pausing before entering, she glanced up. She loved this house, always had. Dearborns had built it a century before. With its four chimneys and multiple roofs and gothic turrets, it wasn't quite a castle but almost. As a young girl she'd fantasized about beauty and perfection, formed by the gorgeous home surrounding her. The house itself had always given her a sense of security, especially when real life hadn't been that easy when she was a kid.

She let herself in, calling, "Mom! Dad! I'm home!"

Funny, but she'd been sleeping so often at Color that she'd practically forgotten this was technically still her address. Her mom rushed out of the living room, her heels clattering on the parquet floor. At a glance Emma could see she was sober, which was both a relief and a surprise. But Diana was usually impeccably groomed, and today her white linen slacks and top looked slept in, her hair in disarray. "I called and *called* you. Why didn't you answer?"

"But I did, Mom. I left a message that I'd be here this afternoon. I knew you'd be upset over the breakup, but it also wasn't something we could discuss in a quick phone call. I had a meeting this morning and then I had to have lunch with Felicity to start calling off all the wedding arrangements—"

Her mother waved a frantic hand, clearly expressing that those were unnecessary details. "You *have* to get Reed back. Right now, today. Immediately. You have to marry him. David!" she called, although she never took her eyes off her daughter. "Emma, you *have* to listen to us!"

Emma stiffened, losing some of the sureness she'd felt walking in here. Her time with Garrett suddenly seemed a million hours ago. "Mom, I know how fond you are of Reed. And I know how much you wanted to have the wedding here, but I'll take care of canceling all those arrangements and details—"

"It has nothing to do with the arrangements or expense, you foolish, foolish girl. David!"

Her father showed up in the doorway. She got a quick hug. Very quick. They got just close enough for her to feel his poker-straight spine, to see the tight lines around his eyes. "Honey, you don't realize what you've done."

"Of course I do. I called off an engagement."

"You threw away a fortune," her mother said furiously. "Now come in here and sit down. After we talk, you can call Reed and make it up to him."

Something was wrong. Nothing they were saying was making sense. The serenity she'd walked in with completely deserted her. "What on earth are you talking about?"

They flanked her going into the living room. Unlike a normal afternoon in this coral-and-cream room, though, there was no decanter of scotch on the priceless Chinese mirrored coffee table, no TV on broadcasting the news, no fancy hors d'oeuvres to munch on. In fact, the room was so still, it resembled a showpiece.

"Sit," her father ordered.

They all did, but it was her mother who started talking. "You've thrown away millions of dollars," she said dramatically.

It was her mom's mom, the Soule side of the family, who'd come over on the *Mayflower*. Her dad had married into that old aristocracy—and old money. His side was hardly poor, and heaven knew, he'd made his own fortune.

But it was the old Soule money that added up to a piece of the rock. At least, the Dearborn rock.

"Come on, you two. Fill me in. I don't have a clue what you're talking about."

"Emma, you claimed for years that you had no interest in marrying. Your grandmother was afraid you meant it. So were we. And there'd be no one to pass on the whole Dearborn legacy unless you married and had children. So your grandmother made it a condition of your trust…that you had to marry before the age of thirty to get the money."

For the first time Emma started to believe that her parents weren't just giving her attitude and dramatics. "Wait a minute," she said quietly. "Just slow down. No one ever told me any of this before—"

"We didn't think we *had* to, honey. Because once you started seeing Reed, we both could see that relationship was becoming serious. If you just go through with the wedding, everything will be fine. I know you hadn't set a firm date, but it was always going to be at the end of July or early August. Definitely before your thirtieth birthday. So all you have to do is follow through—"

"Whoa. Just hold on." Emma stood up, still trying to grasp this.

She'd been a teenager when her grandmother died, and that was the first she'd been told about the trust—and the considerable size of the trust. That security had affected every choice she'd made as an adult. "Grandma didn't know I didn't plan to marry. I was just a kid—"

"But you always talked that way, Emma. The only time it was different was when you were with the Keating boy. But as a child—and after you and Garrett split up—you always sang the same tune. About not wanting to marry. Not needing to marry. And your grandmother—"

Emma heard that out. "All right—but if the trust doesn't go to me, who does it go to?"

"Your grandmother made a list of charities and causes, if you failed to marry. It's all legal. Of course, you could fight it, but the attorneys told us frankly that you'd have no legal ground—"

"There's nothing I'd want to fight," Emma said quietly. "If that's what my grandmother wanted, it would seem she made her choices."

"Don't be ridiculous, Emma," her father said heavily. "Just call Reed. Whatever rift you had, I'm sure it's mendable. You're both reasonable people, hardly children anymore. Everyone has arguments. I can't imagine either of you doing something that wasn't redeemable."

Her dad's voice seemed to fade, as if he were talking from a distance. She saw his lips moving, saw her mother's lips moving.

They were both talking to her at the same time, quickly and urgently.

Emma had the sudden foolish feeling that someone had just smacked her upside the head. No one had, not physically. But the shock of it all finally sank in.

If she didn't marry before her thirtieth birthday, she'd lose everything. Color. She knew how much money she owed on the gallery, knew it still wasn't paying for itself—not the way she'd chosen to run it. All this time, she'd thought she could indulge her belief that the gallery was for the community's benefit instead of for chasing a profit. She'd wanted to expose Eastwick to new artists and new ideas, to all kinds of art and beauty, even if those choices didn't pay her back financially. She could have run the gallery differently, but she'd been so positive she had that massive trust fund coming to support it and herself.

And all this time she'd happily volunteered with troubled teenagers through Eastwick Cares and the little kids through the grief center. Because of her financial security, she'd been able to give her time without worrying about getting paid.

Her clothes, her jewelry, the skiing week in Vail and renting a yacht in Italy…for sure, she'd lived indulgently. But there'd never been a reason to budget. Or to learn how to budget. If she hadn't lived so darn extravagantly, maybe she'd have the money socked away to save her gallery and everything else. But she didn't. Because she'd never thought she needed to.

She lifted a hand in a gesture asking her parents to stop talking. She couldn't hear them anyway. She couldn't seem to hear anything right now, except for the thudding drum in the pit of her stomach. "I need some time to think about this," she said. "I'm going to go upstairs now."

She didn't wait for them to agree or not, just left the room. Until she reached the bottom of the stairs, she wasn't aware her father had followed her. David touched her shoulder to make her turn around.

"Emma," he said quietly, "I just don't understand how you could be so selfish."

"Selfish?" The accusation confused her, when she was the one who'd just had her whole life thrown in the wind. But of course, that wasn't completely true. "Dad, I realize that calling the wedding off is upsetting for you and Mom.

But the marriage would have been a terrible mistake. Neither of us was going to be happy."

"Maybe you believe that. But if you can't be happy with a good man, maybe you damn well better redefine happiness. No one gets everything they want in life."

He sounded more like an army commander than a father. But then, he always had. And as always, she could feel her stomach knotting up. "I never thought that," she said quietly and tried to turn away—but her father wasn't through.

"We've supported you in everything you ever wanted. Your education. Your art gallery. Have you ever asked me for anything I didn't willingly give you? And your mother. Were you even thinking of her? Mark my words, Emma. If your mother goes on another binge, it'll be on you."

This time it was her father who whipped around and strode away from her.

For the second time in two days she found her nerves jittery and her head pounding. She climbed the stairs, hoping that if she just sat alone, she'd get a better grip…. A good theory, but it didn't work worth beans.

Her suite of rooms was decorated in apricot and taupe. Several years before, her mother had surprised her by redoing the rooms. The furnishings were elegant and expensive and thoughtfully chosen. They just weren't colors or furniture that Emma would ever have chosen. Yet she'd never objected, because who knew what was going to send her mom climbing back into a bottle.

Emma sank on the double bed, feeling disoriented… and unaccountably angry. All her life she'd been the peacemaker in the family. All her life she'd tried never to rock the boat, especially because the threat of causing her mother to drink was ever-present. She was on the fund-raising committee at the club because her mother wanted a Dearborn doing that prestigious job. She'd never moved completely out of the house because her mother claimed to need her, claimed she couldn't bear up to David's critical, judgmental attitude. Her father counted on her to be hostess for all the Dearborn social events because they were both wary of any pressure put on Diana.

Emma closed her eyes, feeling the thick humid air drifting from the west window. The frightening part was that the threats were always true. A hundred times Emma had told herself that her parents needed to resolve their problems between themselves. But the same thing happened over and over—when Emma failed to step in, didn't intervene when her mother needed help or play diplomat between her parents, her mom *did* tumble down the alcoholic hill again.

In the last two days Emma had tried to do the wild thing and change roles. Take charge of her life. Stand up for herself. Redefine what was important to her.

The result seemed to be a complete shambles. The latest—the loss of her trust fund—kept slapping in her mind like mini shock waves. It wasn't wealth that mattered to her, but the trust fund had represented security. Independence. Freedom.

Now she opened her eyes, looked around the pale apricot walls and felt them closing in on her.

This morning she'd discovered the wonder, the joy of being wildly in love. But now those moments with Garrett seemed as if they'd taken place on another planet. Claustrophobia seemed to lock the air out of her lungs. She felt so trapped she could hardly breathe. She squeezed her eyes closed, trying to get a grip. Her world had just been completely tipped on its axis, so naturally she felt thrown. Only this was more than *thrown*.

She had no idea what to do next.

She only knew that she felt completely alone. And lost.

Before turning in the driveway of the Baldwin mansion, Garrett stopped at the roadside and used his cell phone to call Emma.

The first two times he'd called, he'd gotten Josh at Color. Josh had promised to leave a message for Emma on her desk, but he didn't know her schedule. Nothing odd about that. Emma was a busy woman. But this was the third time Garrett had been unable to reach her.

He told himself it was idiotic to worry. It was just that this morning… Hell, he was still high from last night and this morning. Obviously making love with a woman right after she'd broken an engagement was terrible timing. But he'd never before felt euphoria like this. A connection like this. A kite-high, heart-soaring thrill of a feeling like this.

For a long time he'd believed that selfish, driven workaholics like himself were doomed to be single. What woman would want them? They were annoying personalities.

But damn, she hadn't made him feel annoying. She'd made him feel like the most powerful, sexy lover in the universe—past and present. And no, he hadn't gone plumb off the deep end and assumed she was ready to marry him.

But in his gut, that *was* on his mind. The M word. He'd never wanted it before, never felt the need or push. But suddenly he couldn't get that hope out of his head, and Emma was the difference. Emma was…

Stop this, he mentally ordered himself. He pocketed his cell phone, climbed out of the car and strode up to the front door of Bunny Baldwin's mansion. He didn't want to stop thinking about Emma, but he still had miles to go this day. Obsessing about Emma wasn't helping. Until he got those tasks done, he couldn't see Emma anyway.

He knocked on the door, waited. Moments later, a tidy gray-haired woman answered. "Can I help you?" she asked.

"You're Edith Carter?"

"Yes."

"Mrs. Carter, I don't need to come in. I realize you don't know me, but I was told you were Bunny Baldwin's housekeeper for years." The gentle-eyed woman nodded. "I'm Garrett Keating."

Immediately she relaxed. "Of course. I know the Keating family. For a moment, I was afraid you were another one of those reporters, trying to dig into more of Mrs. Baldwin's private life."

"No, honestly. I only stopped because I hoped there was a chance you might know something about my sister, Caroline Keating-Spence. She's been in the hospital. I've been trying to put together a picture of what happened in the weeks before she got so sick, and no one seems to know anything. I heard Caroline was often over here—"

Edith nodded, looking thoughtful. "Yes, she was. She and Abby—Mrs. Baldwin's daughter—were friends. The whole group of Debs came over quite often. Bunny loved having the girls around."

"Did you happen to hear anything about my sister? Any gossip or bad news, anything at all?"

"You sound so worried, Mr. Keating," she said compassionately. "I wish I had some information for you."

"But you don't?"

Edith hesitated. "I don't know if you knew my Bunny, but she was interested in everything happening in Eastwick. Some said she was nosy, but the truth was that she simply cared about everything and everyone. I don't know where she got all her news, but by and by, she just seemed to know everyone's secrets. That's how she came to write the *Eastwick Social Diary*."

"Yes," Garrett said, wishing this had to do with his sister but not seeing how.

"Well, the thing is, now all those diaries are missing. Her daughter, Abby, thinks there was information in those journals that someone might have killed her mother for. The police are looking into it. There's no proof. Yet. But…"

Garrett waited.

"I'm just saying, Mr. Keating, that if those diaries would just surface, you might find something about your sister…or someone related to your sister. Something that might be the source of her problem. Because if something was going on in Eastwick, Bunny knew it."

"But right now you don't know where those diaries are."

Edith shook her head. "I'm sorry. No one does."

Once warmed up, Edith went on and on. She'd obviously deeply cared about her employer and needed to tell someone how traumatized she'd been by Bunny's death. Apparently Bunny had been only fifty-two, healthy and full of energy. Although she'd loved gossip, she'd never been vicious.

"Never, Mr. Keating," Edith vowed. "Yes, she dished the dirt on the well-heeled. But she never told a lie, never invented or embellished. She only told the truth. And personally I think she made a huge effort not to hurt anyone who might have been innocent."

"I'm sure she did," Garrett agreed, although he was starting to feel desperate that he was ever going to escape. He'd hoped he'd hear something, anything, about his sister Caroline, but Edith seemed fixed on the night her employer had died.

"I found her, I did. Still haven't gotten over the shock, probably never will. In my head, I still see her lying there. I was right upstairs, putting away linens in the upstairs closet, when I suddenly heard this thud. As if a chair had been knocked over. That kind of thud—"

"I understand," Garrett said swiftly.

"Well, that thud was my Bunny. Lying on the floor in the study. It just didn't make sense." Tears welled in Edith's eyes.

"It sounds horrible." Garrett tried to sound sympathetic.

"Oh, it was, it was. I can't get it out of my mind. And I've stayed on in the house because Abby asked me to. Abby's her daughter, of course, I think I told you that—"

"Yes, I knew that."

"Well, no one knows what's going to happen to the Baldwin mansion yet. So it still needs caretaking. And right now I don't think anyone else would want to live here because of what happened. I hardly do myself, because everywhere I turn, I remember her lying in the study like that. She was more than an employer, you know. She was a friend. A fascinating person. It's unbelievable that someone would kill her. Actually murder her. I keep trying to imagine what kind of secret she knew that was *that* bad—"

He turned the key on his car engine, grateful to be free. Yet listening to Edith had put an edgy beat in his pulse. He'd never personally known Bunny Baldwin, was hard-pressed to invest interest in a woman who'd lived for gossip. But the secret business worried him, because his sister was obviously hiding some kind of secret that had caused her depression—and her feeling of guilt.

He'd checked out Edith, knowing that woman was a long shot, but he was starting to get damned desperate. No information seemed to surface about his sister. He needed to help Caroline, needed to know she was safe, before he could possibly move back to New York.

Instead he seemed to be getting more and more embroiled in Eastwick—which he swore he'd never do.

Halfway down the street, he pulled off to dial Emma again.

Still no answer. That didn't mean she wasn't there, of course. She could have turned off the ringer, simply because she had a busy day. He now had a good idea how busy she really was, how crowded her life was.

Still, he wanted to hear her voice. Wanted to talk to her.

Wanted to know she was okay after making love.

Wanted to know how he was going to react after hearing her voice again.

Garrett told himself he was just frustrated he hadn't reached her, not worried. One way or another, he was determined to contact her today, though, even if he had to track her down all the way to Timbuktu.

More immediately, though, seeing his sister had to be

his first priority. Caroline was getting sprung from the hospital—against his better judgment.

He found her still in her hospital room but sitting up, all dressed and chomping at the bit. "You said you'd be here by three!"

"And it's a quarter to."

"I know, I know. But I started to worry that you wouldn't come. I just want to go home, Gar." She wrapped her arms around his neck for a hug and promptly started crying. Hell and double hell. She felt skinnier than a reed, and he hated it when his sister cried. He always wanted to fix the problem. Right now. Yesterday.

"Would you quit it?" A guy could talk to his sister that way. When she didn't immediately quit—Caroline had never listened to him—he patted her back, over and over. And over.

Finally she quit snuffling and stepped away. He handed her a tissue—she never had one. "Get me out of here," she begged him.

"I will. But you have to do the wheelchair thing."

"That's stupid. I'm not sick."

But her spirit was sick. He could see the darkness behind her eyes, in the nervous way she moved, in the exhaustion in her posture—even when he was wheeling her downstairs and bundling her—and five million flowers—into the car.

"Griff's due home tomorrow," she told him.

"I know. The parents told me,"

"I don't want him to know…about the suicide attempt."

At least she was using the word now. "Caroline, come on. You surely realize that Mom and Dad already told him. They had to give him a reason to cancel his trip and fly home."

"But I didn't want him to do that! And they should have asked me before calling him!"

Garrett didn't try arguing with her. The subject was too sticky to begin with. Truthfully, their parents hadn't asked Griff to come home for their daughter's sake so much as they'd hoped Griff would *do something* about Caroline to stop all the talk. God forbid anyone in Eastwick should discover that Keatings had troubles just like everyone else.

"The thing is, I want Griff to hear about this from *me*. Before he hears it from strangers or the Eastwick gossipmongers— Wait a minute. Who's that woman? What's going on?"

"That woman," Garrett said, "is Gloria." As they walked through his sister's front door, Garrett braced for trouble as he introduced his sister to the woman he'd hired. Gloria was dressed to look like a housekeeper, but essentially Garrett had hired her as security until Caroline's husband actually arrived home and took charge.

No matter what Caroline said or thought, there was no way he was leaving her alone. Not after a suicide attempt. Period. As far as Garrett was concerned, that was the end of the argument—but a half hour later, Caroline was still giving him grief.

By then he'd installed her on the couch in the den with the remote, a cup of tea and a frantically lonesome bichon frise with the ghastly name of Bubbles. Garrett disappeared from sight for a few minutes while Caroline and Gloria started talking, giving them a chance to get to know each other.

As he wandered around, he remembered how much he'd always loved Caro's place. She loved rich, deep colors—burgundies and emeralds and teals. She always chose furniture a guy could sink into, made things comfortable. He never had to kick off his shoes, never had to fret if he was going to spill anything. She was flexible in so many ways, but man, when she played the stubborn card, it was damn hard to budge her.

When he had her alone in the den again, the same fight started up—but this time Garrett dug in his heels. "Look, Griff's coming home, which means you're out of time, kiddo. It's got to come out, whatever the hell trouble you're in. So out with it—and this time I mean it. I'm not leaving until you talk."

She shook her head, the tears already welling up. Her crying made him feel lower than mud. "Caro. This is stupid. What could you possibly have done to feel so guilty?"

He racked his brain for the kind of shameful thing that was so big she couldn't tell him. "A gambling addiction, something like that?"

"For heaven's sake. Of course not."

He frowned. "Could you have stolen something—?"

"Oh, for God's sake, Garrett. You know I'd never do that." Finally he pestered her enough that she came out with it, although her tone had lowered to the most painful of whispers. "I had an affair."

He sank down on the ottoman next to her, relieved to finally have the secret out in the open. "Okay. That's lousy. About the last thing I'd expect you to do, knowing how strongly you feel about fidelity. But all the same...I still don't understand how you get from a mistake to feeling driven to a suicide attempt."

Her eyes started glistening again. "Because I'm in love with Griff. My own husband. How crazy is that?"

Garrett wished Emma were here. She'd know how to handle a conversation like this. He sure as hell didn't. And now that Caroline had turned on the faucet, she finally willingly spilled more. They'd had trouble in their marriage, which Garrett already knew. But they'd mended the breach. And now they were like newlyweds again. In love. Deliriously happy.

"I would never cheat on him now, Garrett. But at the time, I thought we were separated. Fighting. I was certain we were headed for divorce court. It was still a stupid thing to do, sleeping with someone I barely knew, but—"

Garrett didn't need any more details. "So this was when you two were separated—"

"Exactly. But if Griff finds out…" She shook her head. "I *know* how he'll feel. Everything we've built back up will be destroyed. We're both trying hard, and it's working. But if there's a trust issue like that, I know I'll lose him." Out poured the tears again.

"Wait a minute, wait a minute," Garrett said. "Why does he ever have to know?"

And then, finally, came the crux of the crisis. "Because I'm being blackmailed. That's why I took the pills. Because I can't keep paying. And I can't let Griff know. So there's no way out of this, Garrett."

Shock locked his tongue—but only for a second. "The hell there isn't. Who's blackmailing you? *Who,* Caroline?"

She either didn't know or she wouldn't say. Garrett wanted to focus totally on the blackmailer but realized damn fast that that wasn't an option. Right now his sister's frail mental state was more important.

"Caro," he tried to tell her, "Griff knows you. He knows

your background. Our parents were hardly role models for a loving relationship or a marriage, now, were they? I think Griff will understand. He sure as hell won't like it. But if he knows you at all...if he loves you any way it matters...it'll be all right."

She seemed calmed down before he left. But by the time he was walking back to his car, the sun was dipping in the west, a shivery breeze chilling the air.

It was true, what he'd said to Caro. Their parents had been rotten role models. Neither he nor Caro had felt loved or protected as kids. Their parents were devoted to each other on the surface, but their values were all tangled up with influence and affluence and what others thought of them. It wasn't the kind of love Garrett had ever wanted—in fact, he'd always associated marriage with a more painful loneliness than being alone.

He didn't know that had changed until coming home. Until reunited with Emma. Until *being* with Emma, really being with her like last night.

Through all the stresses and strains of the day, a handful of *maybes* kept whispering in his mind. Maybe he could be more than a moneymaking machine. Maybe he could have a private life, be successful in a relationship, create a different kind of marriage...with the right woman.

It was crazy to hope, but there it was. Being with Emma had put the seed in his mind, his heart, and damned if he could stop it from growing.

The instant he got behind the wheel and started the engine, he dialed her cell phone again. This time, *finally,* he caught up with her.

He didn't waste time on greetings or chitchat. Just said

swiftly, "Thank God I finally reached you. I'll be there in ten minutes, fifteen max, Emma."

And then he shot out of his sister's driveway and into the night.

Nine

Garrett turned the corner toward Color and felt his stomach drop. Although it wasn't that late in the evening, he assumed the gallery would be closed and he'd be able to catch Emma alone. Instead, every light in the place seemed to be blazing.

As he strode up the walk, it was pretty damn obvious there was some kind of major event going on. When he pushed open the front door, he suffered an immediate guy panic attack. .

The gallery lobby was packed with women, most of them dressed up and exuberantly waving around wine-glasses. The scents of heavy, expensive perfumes were enough to choke a guy. A few said hello, but most were too intent on their gabfest to pay any attention to an intruding male—which was fine by Garrett.

Initially he couldn't figure out what the big to-do was

about, but once he threaded past the clutch of hard-core drinkers at the wine table, he could see the gallery was hosting some kind of perfume display. At least, there were old perfume bottles all through the front parlor and lobby.

He debated escaping—Emma obviously needed him around right now like she needed a hole in the head. But this couldn't last forever. It was nearly nine, and the gallery normally closed at eight. Besides which, Emma had to be dead on her feet after yesterday's incredibly long hours, so he figured she could use some TLC when this shindig was finally over.

He stuck his hands in his pockets, eased as far away as possible and feigned interest in the perfume-bottle displays. After a few minutes, he didn't have to fake it.

He just checked out a few. Arden Blue Grass, 1934. Myon Coeur de Femme, 1928. Gabilla La Violette, 1912. Lavin L'Ame, 1928.

The price tags made him wonder why he bothered with investment banking when a bunch of old bottles were worth so much. As far as art went, he liked finger painting more— but clearly that opinion was in the minority in this crowd. He ambled farther, just looking and poking around, until he finally spotted Emma.

Damn, but a single look and his throat went whiskey-dry.

How she could still be on her feet and looking this good confounded him, but she was a tender feast for his eyes. She wore a long skirt, some fabric with a sheen, claret in color with some gold-threaded design near the ankles. He didn't normally notice stuff like that, but somehow with her, he found himself noticing everything, because every detail was so much a part of her. The white blouse was simple, billowy, open at the throat to show off a triple strand of pink pearls. She'd left her hair loose, just brushed it back with a pearled clip on one side. She'd smudged a little satiny stuff around her eyes, used a ripe plum color on her mouth. If she was going for a peasant effect, it sure failed. She not only looked beautiful and striking but also elegant to the bone.

In the few minutes he'd wandered around, he'd figured out some things. Not just that old perfume bottles sold well. But also that the crowd was buzzing less about the event than about Reed.

So the vultures had come to peck about the broken engagement—at least when Emma was out of sight. The next time she ambled through the lobby, she spotted him immediately.

The look in her eyes put a hush in his pulse. She surged toward him as if thrilled to see him…but then he saw her swallow and noticed her posture tense with anxiety.

Something was wrong. Very wrong. But before they could connect, she was distracted by Josh, who was apparently leaving for the night. And then a phone call snagged her attention. One way or another, it seemed as if everyone wanted a piece of her.

He'd been in such a hot rush to tell her about Caroline. Still was. Still wanted her perspective on the whole blackmailer mystery as soon as he could get it.

He'd been in an even hotter rush just to see her. To touch her. To find out if last night had been as powerful—and terrifying—for her as it had been for him.

But it took another twenty minutes before she'd managed to shoo the last Eastwick matron down the front steps. By then, he'd had more time to study her, more time to see the strain on her face and to catch the tremble in her fingers. Emma wasn't just tired. She was hiding it well, but clearly she was stressed, only functioning because she was too stubborn to crash. It wasn't hard to guess that the breakup with Reed had spread through the town faster than ants at a picnic. She probably hadn't had an instant's peace all day.

The gallery echoed with an odd sense of stillness. Garrett felt his smile hesitate, an uneasiness pluck his heartbeat. She just looked at him when she locked the door. He saw her hunger to see him…but he also saw even more anxiety in her face.

It was okay, he wanted to tell her. He'd help her weather the gossip about her ex. But right then she seemed strung too tight to talk. As far as he could tell, she didn't need more stress or seriousness right now. She just plain needed a break. So he kept it light.

"I haven't been this scared in a long time," he said wryly. "I thought they were going to riot over a few of those bottles. If you mentioned you had a big event going on tonight, it really slipped my mind."

"I didn't mention it because it wasn't supposed to be a big event. There's a hard-core perfume-bottle-collector crowd in Eastwick, so I just do this every few months. To be honest, I'd all but forgotten it was scheduled because normally it doesn't take much to prepare for it."

"Ah. They just wanted to drink your wine and get a look at you because of the broken engagement?"

"Don't feel *too* sorry for me. One of those bottles sold for two hundred and seventy-five thousand dollars. It was a consignment deal, but still. I'll get my cut."

"Did I hear you right? One of those old, used bottles actually went for 275K?"

When she nodded, he mimicked a man suffering from shock and gasping for air. Though she obviously was not in a laughing mood, her lips tipped and a helpless chuckle emerged. Finally that terrible stiffness eased in her shoulders.

"Oh, Garrett, darn it, I've needed to talk to you all day, but it's been one thing after another. When I finally got a free minute this afternoon, this gallery event exploded on me. But I have something I absolutely need to tell you—"

"And I want to hear it. But not here, Emma." He tried to steer her toward the door, but she balked.

"What's wrong with here?"

"Nothing, normally. But right now your whole gallery smells like a perfume factory. In fact, I think the perfume's destroyed all the oxygen in the entire county."

She chuckled again but still wouldn't budge. "It's not that I don't want to disappear with you—but I can't leave this mess."

Of course she couldn't, he thought. She could hardly open the gallery in the morning with wineglasses and bottles all over the place.

Garrett realized, not too comfortably, that he was completely unused to thinking of other people, their needs, their life details.

But he wanted to change that. While she gathered and locked up all the fragile bottles, he headed for the kitchen. Tackling the dirty glasses and party debris was easy enough. He'd never liked KP—who did?—but he found himself whistling as he threaded the glasses in the dishwasher.

Helping her felt natural. Even more shocking was discovering that being himself with her felt natural. Who'd have believed it? That Emma seemed to just like being with him. That finger painting with her as if he were a little kid had actually been fun. And sex, of course, had been beyond great…but coming alive with her also never had the performance issues that sex and life always did. Somehow, he realized, he just felt *right* with her.

She showed up in the kitchen and grabbed a dish towel.

"Maybe it's as simple as trust," he mused.

"Huh?"

"It's a meaner world than it used to be. Not easy to trust. Not easy to find other people with integrity. And I admit, it's probably always been harder for me to take a chance."

"Okay," she said patiently, "you've obviously been sampling the wine while you handled the glasses—"

He kissed her on the nose, teased the dish towel out of her hand and this time seriously whisked her toward the door. The cleanup was ninety-nine percent done. Enough. "You, cookie, have had more than your share of nonstop running today. Let's get you away from the gallery and phones and see if we can find some food to shovel into you, okay?"

"Cookie?"

"I know, I know. I can't imagine why I called you *cookie*, either. I must be out of my head. In fact, I know I am. I think over you." He said it lightly, so as not to scare the complete hell out of her. And although she shot him a startled look, by then he was switching off the last of the lights, swinging the door closed and then hooking an arm over her shoulder— because the night air was colder than a well digger's ankle.

"You look gorgeous," he said.

"Okay. No more wine for you. Maybe ever."

It felt good. More than good. Getting her smiling, laughing, easing up. And she was way too whipped to give him much trouble by then. He easily bossed her around at his place, got her installed on the couch with a pillow behind her back. Within minutes, he'd handed her a fancy sandwich heaped with cheese and fresh tomatoes and cold cuts, all spilling out the sides and making her chuckle again. The glass, the pillow, the plate the sandwich was on were all hers—things she'd brought over to make this rental place livable.

But she was the one who made it livable. Curled up on that old couch, she brought life and emotion to the place. Still, every few minutes she kept remembering the refrain to her earlier song, and then her good humor would die again.

"Garrett…I really *do* need to tell you something."

"I know you do. You keep saying. And I want to hear. But first explain to me how or why anyone would pay so much for a bunch of used perfume bottles." Before he settled down with her, he turned off the phone, the fax, all the electronics that he usually kept on 24-7.

"I'm not sure I can explain. Perfume bottle collecting is kind of a unique addiction, but if you're not into it—"

"Trust me. I'm not. And likely won't be."

She chuckled again. "Poor baby. Those women really scared you, didn't they? You never saw women in a shopping frenzy before?"

At the end of the couch, he pulled off one of her sandals. Then the other. "Not that close before." He shuddered. "I wouldn't want to get between one of those women and the bottles they wanted."

"It's a lost world now, but there was a time when

perfumes had artists hand make bottles for their product. Once perfumers started using plastic-tipped stoppers, the bottles were never the same. But before that, the really great perfumes all had bottles that were hand designed, truly works of art—" She seemed to hear herself talking— or maybe she suddenly realized he was running his hands up and down the soles of her bare feet. Her throat suddenly flushed with awareness, arousal. Her eyes ducked from his, and she swiftly swung her legs over the side of the couch and stood up.

"I know what you're thinking—" she began.

"What gave it away? I was trying my damnedest to make you believe I was fascinated about the bottles."

But this time she didn't smile. "Garrett…I really need to get something off my chest."

The hell she did. She'd had enough stress and crap over the last twenty-four hours to last a lifetime. And all he had to do was gently tug her hands and she promptly folded into his arms. She wasn't that small, but barefoot now, she had to tilt her head back to get kissed. At least to get kissed the right way—where he took her mouth and kept it. Possessed it. Seduced it. Until his head was reeling and she was breathless.

When he let her up for air, her luminous eyes met his and she started to speak…or tried to.

So he had to kiss her again, much more seriously.

He'd been without her all day. Too long. A thirty-five-year-old man should have had years of experience with women to learn self-control, but he didn't. He had more self-control than any twenty men he'd ever met. But not the experience with women.

At least not with women he trusted down deep. Maybe he should have realized how much she mattered when they were teenagers…but for damn sure, he knew how much she meant to him now. His head spun as he kissed and kissed and kissed her yet again. He took a cherishing nip from her neck. Then her earlobe. Then indulged in a long, slow, tongue-stealing kiss, after which he tasted the exquisitely soft length of her throat.

Hell, if she hadn't made a fierce groaning sound of surrender, he probably could have experimented with a thousand more kisses just on her face and neck alone.

Exploring Emma was the most fascinating job he'd ever come across…although Garrett discovered that undoing Emma was an even more consuming occupation.

The pearl clip in her hair had to be jettisoned first, because he needed to be able to freely run his hands through her thick, lustrous hair. The better to hold her. The better to kiss her thoroughly. The better to explore the sensation of her hair sliding through his fingers.

As soft as the texture of her silky blouse was, her skin beneath it was a thousand times softer. He suffered the shock of discovering the wicked woman was wearing no bra beneath it. Imagine. His elegant never-break-a-rule Emma failing to wear a bra, and for that he did his best to reward her.

She seemed to appreciate his tribute, because the tips hardened and the soft white flesh swelled and tightened under the cup of his lips, under the wash of his tongue, under the caress of his palm. She sucked in breath after breath. Her hands by then were busy, too, pulling at any clothes she could reach, at his shirt, the buttons.

Heaven knew, he wanted his clothes off, too, preferably faster than yesterday, but he was determined to hold on to some control. He hadn't even gotten her into the bedroom yet. The soft mattress, the darkness, was only a room away.

She'd had a traumatic day, and her ex still had to be on her mind. Before making love, he didn't want anything on her mind—but him. And them. And what they brought each other.

Not that a guy couldn't tease his lady before going for the end run. He slipped the blouse off her, whooshed it onto a chair, carefully unclipped each earring, kissing each ear at the same time, then stripped off her rings and wrist bangles. Those took more kisses, more time. She seemed impatient as if she wanted him to rush.

She made him rush, all right. The blood seemed to be shooting in his veins, starting with his head, aiming straight below his belt. Something was weird about her skirt. No snap. No button. Finally he got it, that the skirt had some type of fancy clasp—tricky and confusing for big hands to figure out, so it was a damn good thing he was inspired.

The long claret skirt fell in a swish to her bare feet.

Then the only thing she wore were white underpants—at least he thought the teensy scrap of lace was underpants. And, of course, the triple strand of pink pearls trying to hide between her breasts.

The lace went first. But that was as good as he was capable of being. His patience and control had been too tested.

The pearls were coming to bed with them.

Her arms wound tight around his neck when he lifted her. Her mouth had latched onto his and refused to let go.

He couldn't exactly see. Not that he didn't know where the bed was. Not that he had any intention of dropping her.

Not that he gave a damn whether he could see or not.

He could feel. Her. Feel the weight of her, the textures of her. The beauty of her. Smell her hair, her skin; taste her breath, her mouth, her throat.

He lowered her on the bed, then annoyingly realized he was still wearing pants—and part of his shirt. He shucked both, then came back to her. Finally there was nothing between them but pearls. Bare skin rubbed against bare skin, his erection inspired to make her feel appreciated. She kept making these sounds, these soft, soft sounds of yielding, of yearning, of surrender.

Maybe she wanted to drive him mad. Maybe she could. Maybe she already had.

She gave so willingly. That was what got to him the most. She opened her arms, her legs, her trust for him. As self-contained as he'd always been, Emma had held herself tighter yet—and needed to. He'd learned toughness. She hadn't. He could do cold. Not her.

At least not now, with him. She wrapped her legs snug and high around him, pulling him into her, her palms and fingers gliding all over him, arms, shoulders, back, wooing him deeper into her…and then deeper yet. That sensation of sliding into her was like none other in the universe.

He wanted to stay there, savoring the sensation, for another hundred years. At least for another second. But the need to claim her, to possess her, was a thousand times more powerful. Garrett could have sworn he didn't have a single caveman urge…but it seemed he did. The need to make her his woman, to own her at that instant, was more compelling than any need for air or water. Nothing else would do but having her. Then. Right then. Fast and hard.

"Love," she whispered helplessly.

"I do. Love you," he whispered back.

"Love you. Love *you*," she whispered, and damnation, but that destroyed his last drop of control. They both rode that wave, high, fast, sweat-and-heat fast, silver-fast, climbing until both of them hit the mountain peak at the same time. Then spilled over.

He came and came and came, as if he hadn't had an orgasm in years, as if he had some fierce primal need to fill her up with his seed, his life. She called out and then called out again, until they both finally sank against the pillows, whipped and breathing rough and hard.

She laughed suddenly, softly, as if she couldn't believe the wild, wicked ride they'd just been through together. So did he, kissing her damp forehead, loving the feeling of her in his arms.

For a few minutes he was too beat to move…not that he wanted to. But eventually he realized that her skin was cooling and he shifted up on an elbow just to untangle the blanket and spread it over them. She didn't budge beyond snuggling her cheek more intently into his shoulder.

He had to smile again.

She'd already fallen asleep. He strongly suspected that she'd sleep long and hard if he could ensure she wasn't interrupted.

As crazy as it sounded, he felt as if his life started at this precise moment. Making love the night before had been extraordinary and wonderful…but just now she'd become his woman. Really his. In spite of impossible odds, he'd found the one woman, the only one, who'd ever made him believe in love.

God knows there were troubles ahead. His sister. The craziness of his work, trying to live in two places right now, not being settled. And then there were his faults—the workaholic thing. The self-centered, too-focused thing. The terror that he wouldn't know how to love her the right way, that he'd learned only wrong things from his parents, his life.

But damn, there was time to sweat all of that, and tonight wasn't it.

Right now he had her in his arms. All he wanted. All that could possibly matter.

Ten

Emma kept having the strangest dream—she knew it had to be a dream because she was naked except for a string of pearls.

The dream was the opposite of a nightmare. She was walking out of an ugly tunnel—a dark place where she knew she'd been trapped and anxious and never able to see sunlight. Yet in the dream, the answer was so simple. She followed the path out of the tunnel into another world, a beautiful world, where aspens shivered in the wind, revealing leaves of real gold. The sun bathed down warmth but was never so hot as to burn.

She felt strong and happy and loved....

And then she suddenly opened her eyes. Garrett had pulled a chair next to the bed, was sitting there with a mug between his hands, staring intently at her. "Hey, beauty," he murmured. "I was starting to worry."

"Worry?" she asked groggily.

"I've talked to London twice. Paris once. Switzerland three times. Handled over four million in securities and investments. Had breakfast—"

"Good grief. What time is it?"

"Take it easy." A royal finger ordered her head back down to the pillow. "It's only eight o'clock."

"How could it only be eight, if—"

"No big sweat. All those places are on a time zone that works early in the morning here. If I need to call Tokyo, it's a whole different story."

That was interesting information, she thought. Even fascinating. But the crazy thing was she hoped he'd keep on chitchatting. Just like this. For another few time zones or two. Waking up to him was even better than the dream. How corny was that?

"Note that I didn't climb back into bed with you," Garrett said. "For which I think you should give me at least seventy-five brownie points."

"Because?"

"Because I knew you were exhausted. In fact, you were sleeping so deeply that I kept checking to make sure your heart was still beating."

"That's the most creative excuse I've heard for feeling a girl up."

He nodded solemnly. "It's the best I could come up with on a moment's notice. But if it were up to me, I'd stand guard so you could sleep all day. This kind of tired isn't fair, cookie. You've been carrying too heavy a load. But I wasn't sure if I could let you sleep much longer, because I didn't have any idea what commitments you had today or when they started."

She closed her eyes. "I've got a project I'm involved with for Lily Cartright this afternoon. You know Lily, don't you? She married Jack Cartright, partner in that big law firm? And since Lily's pregnant now—" A cup of tea seemed to have made its way into her hands. She took a sip, found it hot, strong, sweet. Perfect. "She's been farming out projects whenever she can find a—"

"Sucker."

"Exactly. Anyway, she's got a group of troubled kids. Teenagers about age thirteen and fourteen. Not in trouble with the law yet but aiming there—truants, cutting class, that kind of thing."

"Don't tell me you finger paint with them," he teased.

"No. I'm doing a wall with them. A mural. Free-form. Not art exactly but using colors and shapes that work for them. It's their therapy room, so they're creating the whole thing, from floor to ceiling."

"So you get to work with a handful of ornery, belligerent, smart-mouthed defiant teenagers for—"

A bowl of dewy-fresh raspberries lightly sprinkled with sugar appeared on her lap. "A couple hours a week. But Lily needs the help. And they love it, Garrett. How could I say no?"

"You frame your mouth like this." He demonstrated. "It's just a one-syllable word. You used to be great at saying it. Especially to me."

She had to laugh. "That was a different issue, you devil. The kids are great to me. They're no trouble at all."

"I didn't want to be trouble for you when we were teenagers either. I just wanted to get in your pants."

"Well, sheesh. The last couple days, I've let you do anything you wanted. You just had to wait a couple of years before I changed my vote." She added thoughtfully, "Come to think of it, I was stuck waiting a couple of years, too."

"So what do you think? Was the wait worth it?"

"It was more—*more*—than worth it, Mr. Keating. In fact, if you'll climb back under the sheets with me for a couple of minutes, I just might show you how worth it it was. I might even show you what I can do with a fresh raspberry."

"My God. You are trouble." He took the tea, stashed it on the table and then dived for her. Raspberries spilled everywhere. The bowl tipped on the carpet. His arms went around her and he kissed her, winding her on top of him, then beneath. As if all that teasing had been lots of fun…but not half as much fun as the reality of touching her.

Emma hadn't realized any of those truths before. Such as when a man needed to touch his woman, the rest of the world didn't need to exist.

And when a woman needed to touch her man, it was exactly the same.

They tussled and romped and played, until the friction and heat under the sheets caused a spontaneous combustion.

He'd seduced her with infinite patience and sensuality and tenderness the night before, but this morning was a hot, wild ride.

Power outages should have occurred from the amount of sizzling bright lightning between them.

Eventually she crashed against the pillow, all sweaty, an insanely beatific smile on her face, and he crashed on his back, one arm still thrashed over her, as damp as she was, the same beatific smile on his face.

Until his telephone rang.

They both ignored it. Eventually it stopped ringing. Garrett never acted as though he'd even heard it, never stopped looking at her for even a moment.

But the jangling sound slapped her back to reality. For hours she'd completely forgotten the shock and panic of her real reality. "Garrett, I need to tell you something serious."

"Okay."

"I tried to tell you yesterday."

"I know you did. And I never meant to cut you off, Em. I just honestly thought you needed some rest. You've had nonstop stress."

He carved a hand around her temple and cheekbone, smoothing away her damp hair. "It wasn't hard to figure out what you were going through yesterday. I know Eastwick. The whole town found out about your broken engagement and was on your back all day to get the details."

"That's true. In fact, it was the reason I couldn't get time to talk to you yesterday. But that's not the problem I need to share." She took a breath, intent on gathering her thoughts, but he went on, as if believing she needed soothing and reassuring.

"Reed's going to be on your mind for a while. You care for him, cared for him. The town isn't going to let you forget his name right away even if you wanted to. I promise I'm not going to add to that problem for you."

"I didn't think you would—"

Again, he interrupted. "If we come out publicly as a pair right now, the town will think you left Reed for me. I know how they are, believe me." Clearly he'd worried about the kind of issues she had to live with in Eastwick. "So I realize we'll have to be discreet for a while. But I can't imagine either of us wanting to be anything but discreet anyway."

"That's true." She hadn't even thought that far ahead. Garrett obviously had. When she ducked her head, though, his knuckles gently chucked up her chin so their eyes were meeting again.

"Emma. I'm in love with you. It's a new feeling for me. Terrifying and terrorizing. But I know this is right."

A lump filled her throat. A lump both of joy and dread. "I never expected to feel anything like this, either. It was good when we were kids, Gar. But nothing like what I feel for you now."

He nodded. "Still, we can take this as slow as you want. I don't know how to do this courtship thing. So I'll have to learn. I want to do it right. I admit, I'm a slow developer, but honest to Pete, I've got a decent IQ. So if you'll just be patient and not freak out if I do something wrong now and then—"

She sat up, shook up now. "Garrett."

"What?"

"Hush."

"Okay."

"Something happened yesterday. My parents—I knew they wanted to see me. I knew they wanted answers about why I'd broken the engagement to Reed, so I went there." She sighed, then just blurted it out. "I found out I'm going to lose everything."

"Lose what? What do you mean?"

God. It was so good to talk to someone who wasn't

going to heap judgments on her head, who wasn't so close to Eastwick society that he'd be influenced by anything beyond...well, beyond her. "All this time, Garrett, I thought I had a trust fund, set up by my grandmother, that I'd inherit when I was thirty."

"Okay."

"It's hefty. Several million dollars."

"So. That's great."

"The thing is, knowing about the trust fund always affected how and why I live the way I do. I love my gallery, but I always chose what to display, what to sell, not based on a profit but on what I wanted to give to the community. I tried to pick what I thought was beautiful. What I thought added to us all. Not just what would bring me in the mortgage payment."

Garrett didn't interrupt her this time, only listened. But she caught the faintest smile—not patronizing but gentle. When he touched her cheek, she could almost see the opinion in his mind—that she was a hopeless idealist. And that he liked the quality in her.

"It's not just that gallery. But all the volunteer work I do. The projects I take on at the country club are more about my parents than me. Likewise, the hostess chores I do for my dad. But what I do for the kids—I've always volunteered a lot of hours because I never had to worry about income, you know? I always knew I had this tidy little fortune coming in."

"Pretty obviously," he said quietly, "that changed. Somehow."

She sat up, nodded vigorously, wishing she could shake the lump from her throat. "What my parents never told me—until yesterday—was that I had to be married by the age of thirty to inherit that money."

"Say what?" The sudden crease on his forehead registered his confusion. He sat up, taking an immediately more serious posture. It stopped being a snuggle-on-the-pillow conversation once he realized she had a serious problem.

Or that's what she thought was happening. She sat up, too, reached for a long-sleeved shirt of his. She didn't mind being naked with him. In fact, for the first time in her life she felt free to be herself in every way. But the subject was so troubling that she could feel a heart chill settling in.

They both ended up in his tiny kitchen. She curled up in a chair with a fresh mug of tea. He leaned against the counter, looking oddly distant—probably because the sun was behind him at the window, and his face looked more austere and shadowed. "I don't understand. Why would your grandmother have set up the trust that way?"

"It seems that my grandmother—as well as my parents—heard me talk against getting married from the time I was little. To be honest, my parent's marriage was enough to scare anyone away from the institution. And it just seemed so many marriages in Eastwick were about money. Mergers. Conglomerations. Bringing businesses and dynasties together." She swept back her hair with a fretful hand. "I didn't want that."

"Hell, neither did I."

"Anyway…" She sipped, willing the tea to start bracing her. It felt good to get this out in the open. To share the problem with Garrett. To have someone she *could* tell. "I think the idea was to blackmail me into marriage and kids."

"Which is fine—only how was that supposed to work if you didn't know it was a condition of the trust?"

Something in his voice caught her attention. Something *off*. Cool. But when she lifted her head to study him, his expression just seemed...neutral. She assumed she'd imagined that sudden odd tone.

"According to my parents, once I started seeing Reed a couple years ago, they believed we'd end up married. They thought they'd never have to tell me." She shook her head at the black humor of it all. "It's so ironic, because they couldn't *wait* to tell me yesterday. They wanted me to call Reed immediately. Make up with him. They were very, very positive a few million dollars would motivate me to do anything to get him back."

Garrett fell silent.

She didn't know what she expected him to say. Nothing, really. Only his silence seemed to stretch out for an odd length of time. Maybe it was just too much to take in at one time, she thought. But then he asked, "When is your thirtieth birthday?"

"August thirty-first."

"So let me see if I've got this right. If you're not married before August thirty-first, you lose those millions?"

"I don't actually know how much it is. It was three million when my grandmother established the trust. But you know how money well invested can add up." She squeezed her eyes closed for a minute. "I'm having the hardest time just...grasping it. Not the loss of the money so much. But how I'm now facing quite a disaster because I so totally took that inheritance for granted. I never saved, never questioned my financial choices. Spent too much on cars and clothes and anything else I wanted. And now it's a shock. Not just to give up my gallery but not to be able to do all the volunteer work with kids—"

Garrett turned around, plunked his mug down on the counter hard enough to make a slapping sound. "I guess the answer to that is easy enough."

"Pardon?"

"All you have to do is marry before you're thirty, right? Reed wasn't right for you, but it's not like he was your only choice. You had me hooked before you kicked him out of the running."

"Pardon?" she said again, this time more softly.

"I'll marry you, Emma. If you want that money, it's yours. No big sweat."

His voice was as cool as a cucumber on a hot summer day. Dripping cool. Tangy cool. When she didn't immediately respond—at that precise instant, she couldn't get her tongue to form a word if her life had depended on it—he said, "I'm no idealist about money. It's not pretty or romantic to be poor. There's no reason to be embarrassed about wanting to live well. No one throws away a fortune, Emma, it's stupid. You'd be crazy to throw away your independence, your security. Besides, why would you want to do that?"

From one second to the next, she felt as if she'd aged half a century, because she stood up on shaky knees and halting balance. "I wasn't asking you to marry me," she said quietly.

"I know that. But it's a perfectly reasonable solution to your problem. God knows we get along between the sheets. Always did have a click together—" His phone rang. At the same time, his fax started exuberantly frothing out waves of paper. He stepped toward the phone but said to her first, "No reason in hell we can't be married before your birthday."

As he walked across the room, took his business call, for a good sixty seconds she fought for calm. She felt as if someone had punched her in the stomach. She couldn't seem to recover.

She even wanted to laugh. For the first time in her entire life she really did want a marriage proposal. The biggest dream her heart ever had was a proposal specifically from Garrett.

But not like this.

Not because he thought she'd marry him for money.

The funniest, saddest part of it was that Emma had thought—she'd really, really thought—that Garrett cared for her. Even loved her. That he *knew* her, the real Emma, the Emma she rarely showed to anyone, and that that was the woman he'd taken to bed. And maybe even fallen in love with. At least, he'd said he loved her.

But that, of course, was under the covers.

Now she knew better.

He was still on the phone, still talking—in French she thought, without really registering what he was saying. But then, she wasn't registering what she was doing either. Taking steps like a sleepwalker, she strode barefoot toward the door, wearing his shirt, her hair not brushed, her clothes and shoes still somewhere around his place—probably strewn every which way.

She couldn't remember ever doing anything improper in public.

It wasn't that she cared so much what others thought of her but that she never willingly exposed herself that way. Yet she walked out his door and down the sidewalk toward Color dressed like that. Or undressed like that, depending on one's point of view.

Right then, she didn't seem to have a point of view. She just had to get out of Garrett's presence before that punch in the gut caught up with her. The pain was going to hit good. She knew it. But she didn't want him or anyone to see it.

All Emma wanted was to hide out and lick her wounds in private, but life just refused to cooperate. She couldn't let down the teenagers for the afternoon mural project. The gallery still had to be opened and operated. Her telephone never stopped ringing, and although she could have turned off the darn thing, that only avoided problems rather than solved them. Unless she faced people and spoke to them, people could well believe that Reed was responsible for their engagement breakup—especially since the man had apparently disappeared from sight—and it wasn't right having people blame him. And on top of all that, she had a dozen prewedding plans that needed immediate canceling.

So she sucked it up and did the day and tried her hardest to keep her mind off Garrett. But by late afternoon she'd had it. Maybe you could glue a cracked eggshell back together temporarily, but no way could that glue hold forever.

"Josh, you can man the place for a couple hours, can't you? I know Jeremiah isn't here, but I need to disappear in the workshop for a while, get some things ready for the July show."

"Sure, Emma. You want me to tell everyone you're gone for the day?"

Bless Josh. He never asked a personal question. He just seemed to want a job where people left him alone about being gay. In so many ways, she could count on him for discretion. It helped to be able to close the door on the shop and focus on cleaning canvases and frames and organizing display concepts.

She wasn't concentrating well, couldn't pretend to, didn't try.

She just wanted to fill the day's hours and do her damnedest to wear herself out. Barely fifteen minutes passed before there was a knock on the door, though, and it wasn't Josh.

Mary Duvall poked her head in. "Your employee said you were busy and didn't want to be interrupted, Emma."

"It's all right." It wasn't, but Mary was already inside now. And any other time, she'd have been glad to see her old friend.

Mary lifted a satchel of canvases to explain why she'd intruded. "You told me to bring some work if I wanted it in your show. Especially that I needed to bring it before the end of June. So I was afraid if I didn't get around to showing you these, it might be too late for you to even consider them."

"You're so right. Come on in, let's have a look."

Mary stepped in tentatively, studying Emma's face as if unsure if she were really welcome. Emma wanted to shake her head. The Mary Duvall she'd known in school had lots of brass attitude and spunk—of course, life and age changed everyone. But *this* Mary was wearing a subdued denim skirt and basic blouse, no style in sight, and seemed shyer than a wren.

Man, though, her work wasn't remotely shy. As Emma slowly examined the portfolio, she felt distracted for the first time all day. She saw striking colors. Emotion. Vision. Paintings that offered something fresh and thoughtful and deep.

"My God. Why didn't you give me stuff to display before?" Emma scolded her.

"You do want them then?"

"And anything else you've got. I'd love to give you your own show, but right now the best I can do is include you in the July program." She didn't say that she may well need to close the gallery after that. "After that…I don't know, but I'll help you find places to display whatever you have, hook you up with the best dealers. You're wonderful."

They chatted a bit longer. Without thinking, Emma insisted Mary attend the next Debs lunch. Mary had been to one, but Emma sensed she needed more coaxing to feel part of the Eastwick fold again. The words came out of her mouth so easily that she suddenly had to gulp.

Obviously she shouldn't be igniting the old friendship or playing welcoming committee to Eastwick for Mary when she no longer had any idea where she was going to be or what she was going to do—and those decisions were going to slap her in the face awfully fast. Mary had no reason to know about her personal crises, but possibly her expression gave something away, because her old friend's voice turned gentle.

"I expected this would be a bad day to visit, but that's partly why I did, Emma. I'm sure you know that everyone's buzzing about your sudden broken engagement. And it seems like you must be bearing the brunt of the talk alone. I don't know if Reed holed up on his ranch or just plain disappeared for a while, but word has it that he's completely out of sight. Unfortunately that's made the gossipmongers cackle even more."

When Emma didn't respond, Mary said softly, "I don't want to add to all that. I just thought you might need someone around who wasn't going to ask you questions or bug you. It may have been years since I lived in Eastwick, but it's not like I've forgotten how the grapevine works— Aw, hell. Don't, Em. Don't."

Emma wasn't crying. She never cried in public. She knew people thought of her as idealistic, but no one had a clue she'd grown up with an alcoholic parent or anything else that was personally difficult. She'd learned at a young age to keep vulnerability out of sight. It was just…

Nothing seemed important right now. She couldn't care less about gossip and Eastwick. Running the gallery and canceling wedding arrangements and all the other life chores she'd done that day had seemed beyond irrelevant. She couldn't even garner any interest in facing the major life challenges and changes she had to because of losing the trust she'd counted on for so long.

"Oh, Emma…" Mary surged toward her and tried to pull her into a hug. "I understand. It hurts. It doesn't matter who caused the breakup. Breaking up is always horrible. Whatever happened between you and Reed…"

"It's not Reed," she choked out.

"Yeah, right. Like your heart's not broken?"

God, what a mess. Her heart was broken, for damn sure. But not over Reed.

Over Garrett.

Everything else might be life-altering and awful and painful. But the one thing she couldn't imagine getting over was how completely she'd misjudged Garrett. She'd never fallen in love before. Never felt love. Not the way she did for him.

And to have him believe she'd pursued him to get an inheritance?

How could he know her so little? How could he think so little of her?

Eleven

Garrett stood on the tarmac at the private airport in Eastwick, waiting for the Lear to slide to a smooth stop and the doors to finally open.

The sky was fat with muddy clouds, the rain coming down in a steady downpour—matching Garrett's dark mood perfectly.

Still, when the lone passenger clipped down the metal steps from the plane, Garrett hustled toward him. His sister's husband was stocky, with blond hair and weather-ruddy skin, wearing a tropical khaki jacket and chinos that looked well slept in.

"Griff." Garrett extended a hand first. Both were private men and too strong-minded to be close friends, but all Garrett wanted from his sister's husband right now was to be a full-fledged ally.

Griff's expression seemed to echo the same sentiment. "I'm glad it was you who arranged for the private plane and had me picked up. I don't understand what's going on. Your parents haven't told me anything except that Caro was in the hospital."

"Let's get out of the rain. Then we'll talk."

"I haven't slept in almost thirty hours. But I still want to hear—"

"You will." Garrett drove, taking the south road where the highway snaked around curves, revealing views of the pewter bay. The windshield wipers could barely keep up with the steady, slooshing rain.

They passed the road to the Cartright house. After that came the secluded nest of homes that included the Baldwin mansion. In town, even this early in the day, all the store lights and streetlamps were already on because of the dark storm. A crackle of lightning promised more of the same. When they passed the Farnsworth house, Griff finally spoke up.

"You missed the road."

"No. I think we'd better talk before you see my sister."

The rolling country outside Eastwick had clusters of horse farms and stables—and nice little country roads where a car could pull in, cut the engine and not be noticed in the shadow of trees. Garrett put his head back and then just let the truth out. "She tried to commit suicide. Came damn close to succeeding."

"*What*? Your parents told me she was critically ill from some kind of drug interaction. Which is what I found so confusing, because the only medicine I knew she was taking was birth control and an occasional aspirin. What—"

Garrett motioned him to silence. He turned, needing to

look at his brother-in-law, needing to know this man better than he ever had before. "She's not herself, Griff. She's shaky and scared and she needs help. Not someone who's going to crucify her."

"You think I would? Hell, I'd never have left home at all if I'd realized she was depressed." He stared at Garrett. "There's more, isn't there?"

"Yes. Way more."

"Tell me. *Now*. I need to know exactly what's wrong with my wife. And what the hell's going on that no one's given me a straight answer before this."

Garrett didn't move. His brother-in-law's responding with anger was just what he'd have done if someone had dared to keep him in the dark. But he still worried how to handle the situation because he knew tact had never been his strong suit.

"I said, *tell* me. What's going on? I demand to know."

"And I want to tell you because I believe your knowing the whole picture could be a matter of my sister's life. Otherwise I'd never consider breaking her confidence. But I can't give you the whole picture at this exact minute."

"The hell you can't."

Garrett didn't smile, but he almost wanted to. It was so easy to deal with another man. Men understood each other. Men responded in predictable ways.

Men were nothing like Emma.

"This is what I want to do, Griff," he said bluntly. "I need to give my sister a chance to tell you the situation herself. If you still have any questions two days from now, then call me. I promise to fill you in."

"Not good enough," Griff snapped.

"It has to be. Because I won't betray her trust if I don't have to. And right now I don't want to even take you back to her unless I'm damn sure you'll be good to her."

"I love Caroline, for God's sake! Why on earth would you think I wouldn't be good to her? Because we had some trouble a couple years back—"

"No, that's not it." Garrett rolled down a window. Rain whisked in, but it was too hot and too tight in the car without fresh air. For that matter, right now his whole life felt too hot and too tight to breathe. And his sister's mess was only part of it. "It took a long time for me to trust you—"

"That's a likewise. I always thought Caroline loved you more than me."

"She doesn't. She loves you more than anyone or anything in the universe." Garrett said it bluntly, to see Griff's reaction.

"I feel the same way about her." No hesitation. Only increased anxiety. "I *need* to know what's wrong or how can I possibly know what to do or how to help her—"

"And one way or another, you will. I promise. But…Griff, you know our background. Our parents. You know Caroline never had the security of feeling wanted or needed."

"You're not telling me news."

"I'm just saying…she was always more likely to make some mistakes that maybe another woman wouldn't. Not because of lack of character. But because of lack of security, on the inside. And if you can't deal with that, then I'd just as soon take you back to that plane. Fly you anywhere you want to go. Pay your way—"

"Shut up, Garrett. I'm not bribable. I thought you knew that."

Finally Garrett's pulse eased. "I hoped you wouldn't be." He added, "She's scared to see you. Know that. And ashamed of this suicide attempt. Know that, too. And if you didn't guess, our parents heaped more stress—and guilt—on her head rather than less."

"Nothing new there, huh?" Griff said wryly and then sank against the passenger seat as if trying to process all the information and implications just given him. "Get me home, would you?"

"Yes." Garrett, reassured, started the car and aimed toward their house. Barely another minute passed before Griff piped up again.

"What's wrong?"

Garrett glanced at him. "You don't think the scenario I laid out for you was enough?"

"I meant…what's wrong with *you?* You look as if you haven't slept in a week. Business troubles?"

"No." Garrett hesitated. Normally he'd never have confessed a personal problem to anyone. But because he wanted a stronger bond with Griff—and because he felt so damned shattered he couldn't think clearly anyway—he admitted, "It seems that my love life has a lot in common with a train wreck."

"Someone in New York?"

"No. The where of it doesn't matter. The thing is…hell, I guess I just assumed it would never happen to me. That I'd fall, like in the storybooks. I thought the whole thing was a myth. Until…her. I can't believe how the whole world changed, that fast, that completely. Only…"

When Garrett didn't immediately fill in that blank, Griff guessed, "She cheated on you?"

"No. Nothing like that."

"She doesn't care the same way you do?"

"I thought she did." Garrett stopped at a red light, stared dead ahead until it changed. "Now I don't know. I just found out that our getting married could mean a ton of money for her. I understand money. Believe me. And I'd marry her any way she'd have me, to be honest. It's just…I thought her being with me was about—" He couldn't, didn't, say the word *love*. Not to another man. "I thought we were clicking. That we both felt the same thing exploding between us. So it hit me in the gut hard. That there was money behind it."

"You're sure there was?"

"Oh, yeah, I'm sure. She came out and admitted it." Garrett kept replaying the whole thing in his mind. Her sitting there on his chair, wearing his shirt. His feeling so full of emotion for her, love, caring, protectiveness, lust, all of it. And then her so guilelessly spilling the whole story of her suddenly lost inheritance. Her knowing— because she had to know—that he was so wrapped up in her that she could have said anything in the universe to him at that moment.

He could feel Griff's eyes on him. They were only a pinch away from pulling into his sister's driveway. "Hell, that's rough," his brother-in-law said quietly and then slowly added, "It seems ironic that we were just talking about the issues that affect Caroline…and that you're going through something the same way."

"Come again?"

"I meant…I know how you two grew up. That cold household. Your parents into status and the prestige of their social life a ton more than they seemed to care about either of you kids."

Garrett pulled into the driveway, braked. "That's exactly why I need you to be extra good to Caroline. Need you to give her more rope than someone else. She has a ton of love in her, Griff. But I think, coming from where we did, it'd be unrealistic to think she could make a marriage work without getting lost now and then. I don't mean that any-thing's your fault. Or hers. Just that for sure the two of us are stuck with a longer learning curve than most people."

"Yeah," Griff agreed. "That's exactly why I asked if you were positive about that woman's feelings for you. Because possibly the Keating background influenced how you saw the situation."

Garrett saw his sister's face in the living room window, saw Griff's eyes light up when he saw her. When Griff shot out of the car—completely forgetting his luggage— Garrett had to smile, had to believe those two had a real chance at making things right together.

But his smile disappeared as he backed out of the driveway.

His brother-in-law's insight started clawing on his nerves—about his having the same dysfunctional back-ground Caroline did. Garrett knew exactly how relationship-challenged he was. But that sure as hell didn't mean he knew how to fix the shattering mess he'd made with Emma.

Before he could panic, though, he pulled over the side of the road and dialed her cell.

She answered—which was good. But he could hear heaps of noise and other people's voices in the background, as well as the chill in her voice—which wasn't so good.

"Look," he said and then stopped. "I upset you."

"More than upset me."

"I was in the wrong," he said immediately but couldn't very well elaborate because he didn't know exactly what he'd done.

"Not wrong," Emma corrected him. "Not if that was honestly how you felt."

He sensed a terrifying trap and shifted to what mattered. "I want to marry you. That's how I feel. That's what I thought you wanted, too…maybe not that very minute? I assume you'd have wanted to spend more time, have a chance to be more sure. But right then was when the money problem came up."

"Garrett, I didn't tell you about the problem because I was expecting you to solve it. I told you because it was something traumatic that happened to me and I thought—hoped—that you'd become someone I could honestly talk to when there was a problem."

"You can. For God's sake, you can." He pushed on. "Emma, I don't give a damn about money. I've got plenty of money. It doesn't need to be an issue—"

"But it is," she said so softly he could barely hear over the confounding noise in her background. "If you thought I was with you—if you thought that I slept with you—as a way of getting my inheritance, then we're not just worlds apart. We're a universe apart. I'm sorry I misunderstood."

"Emma—" he started to say. But there was no one listening. She'd quietly hung up.

Out of nowhere, the rain had suddenly stopped. Clouds tumbled over each other to reveal patches of azure sky. A bunny peeked out from the woodsy roadside. The afternoon had turned idyllic. Everywhere but inside him.

He'd lost her. He hadn't been dead positive until now, but this conversation sealed what he'd feared all day. He'd blown it. Apparently irreparably. He'd just found her—the one woman who'd made him believe in love, in himself, in a future. And now she was gone.

Without her, he felt a knife twist in his heart, so sharp, so raw, that his incredibly stupid heart actually felt broken. And that's exactly how it was going to be, he feared.

Either he miraculously—quickly—found a way to heal this breach with Emma or neither his life nor his heart would ever be the same.

Several days later Emma slipped into a seat at the Debs' table. The lunch had been scheduled a few days earlier than usual—technically to do a more formal welcome back for Mary Duvall, but Emma had private reasons for wanting this lunch over and out of the way.

After spending the last four days soul- and heart-searching, Emma had discovered all kinds of hidden sides to herself she didn't know she had. Some were pleasant. Some not. But she'd surfaced from all that internal searching, made several painful major life decisions and was ready to act.

This lunch was hardly on the level of huge life changes, but it was still something that needed to be done. The girls all wandered in right at noon. Mary took the seat next to her. Outside, it was hotter than the devil. Harry was polishing glasses behind the malachite bar. Kids screamed out at the pool, and the golfers were hiking in for lunch.

Emma had chosen to wear ice-blue today, just silk slacks and a sleeveless tunic, but she'd added white topaz for jewelry. It was her version of power dressing for a hot day—and she knew she'd be grilled up the wazoo, so there was no way around being in the hot seat today.

Initially, though, the lunch started easily. Harry served a fresh-fruit salad, opened the wine, brought out the cheese and seafood plates. The group had opted for a munch lunch. Felicity had tucked in next to her, Lily across from her, with Vanessa Thorpe and Abby Talbot taking the far ends. Caroline had joined them, her first outing since she'd gotten out of the hospital.

When everyone settled down, Emma proposed a toast to Mary. "We were all so busy talking last time that we never really had a chance to welcome Mary back home. At first she thought she was only coming to take care of her grandfather, but now it looks like she's hoping to stay permanently back in Eastwick. Right, Mary?"

Emma had hoped the group would be distracted by Mary—and they were for a few minutes. But they'd barely finished the first course before the group nose-dived on her.

Felicity led the pack. "Come on, Emma, you *have* to tell us what happened with Reed. No one knows anything! And now he's disappeared for a while, so nobody can ask him. You were the one who never wanted to get married, but then you found Reed and seemed so happy. Come on, what happened?"

The question was exactly what Emma had expected—and why she'd been determined to face this lunch and say what needed to be said. "I'm sorry, everyone, but there was no big, dramatic, scandalous reason for the breakup. I think I realized a long time ago that we cared about each other as friends, which was great but not how two people about to be married should feel."

"So who broke it off? You or Reed?" Vanessa asked.

"Emma, if you weren't aware," Abby poked in, "Reed may be flying under the radar these days, but before that he spread the word it was his fault about the broken engagement. That you didn't do anything wrong. So did he cheat?"

"No, no. Reed didn't do anything wrong."

"That's not what the gossipers are saying. Everybody thinks something big had to have happened to cause such a sudden breakup. So they figure Reed must have done you wrong in some way."

Emma firmly put that to bed. "Well, he didn't. If he's been claiming responsibility, it's only because Reed's always going to do the gentlemanly thing and protect a woman. But this wasn't about either of us doing something wrong."

"I think you broke his heart," Felicity said bluntly.

The accusation stung. It was just so ironic to have to talk about broken hearts when her own was crushed to bits and she couldn't share that knowledge. "Well, I hope I didn't. But for anyone who sees Reed, I hope you'll give him sympathy. The only thing I really regret is that I ever took his ring to begin with, because I know now how completely wrong that relationship was."

"You look pale," Lily Cartright said gently.

"Not sleeping?" Abby guessed.

They let her off the hook. Once they all took a really good look at her, in fact, she got an immediate bossy list of orders about getting more sleep, seeing a doctor, arranging for a massage.

"Okay, that's enough picking on me," she said wryly.

"We've got a lot more to talk about this lunch. Caroline's finally out of the hospital. We should be having a dual celebration for both Mary and Caro."

"To be honest, I have a huge secret to tell you all," Caroline said, then glanced around to ensure no outsiders were close enough to hear this part of the conversation. When she tugged her chair closer to the table, the others pulled up closer, too.

"My husband wanted me to tell you this. So did my brother Garrett, which I'm sure Emma already knows." Caroline took a huge breath. "I've been hiding something from everyone. I was being blackmailed."

"What?" The question echoed through the whole group, everyone expressing shock except for Lily.

"That's why I was so depressed. The blackmailer was threatening me, and I was afraid if the information got out, it would ruin my marriage, my life. But Garrett convinced me to tell Griff. And when Griff got home, I did." Tears welled in Caroline's eyes, but this time not tears of fears or sadness. Tears of relief. "It's been terrible."

"Oh, Caroline." Lily reached for her first. "That's exactly what happened to us. Jack was a blackmailer's target, too. Jack took the blackmail letter to the police a few weeks ago."

"Griff hasn't done that yet. I haven't, either."

"Do it," Lily urged. "Think about it, Caroline. Don't you think it's highly unlikely there could be two blackmailers in Eastwick? So this could well be the same person who was terrorizing us."

Abby suddenly spoke up. "There's a connection between the two. There has to be. Between my mother's mysterious death and the theft of her journals and now two blackmail attempts. Whoever stole those journals is using the information."

"That's what it sounds like," Caroline agreed worriedly. "But, Abby, your mom never published stuff that was so…damaging. She wasn't into cruelty—"

"She published the truth. She never invented anything. But that's part of what I think is the issue. She didn't use everything she knew. There could have been all kinds of things in those journals that no one knew but my mother and, of course, the people involved. And now whoever stole those journals knows that kind of private information, too."

"But who?" Vanessa asked. "It has to be someone in Eastwick. Someone we know. Someone who'd know enough about us all to know what would hurt different people, you know? A stranger couldn't read any stuff like that and know it could cause damage."

"Yikes," Felicity said. "This is getting scarier and scarier. To think that someone we know and trust is the culprit."

"Not just a culprit. A blackmailer and a murderer." Abby drummed her fingernails on the table. "I hate it that you were a victim, too, Caroline. But it makes me feel even more convinced that my mother was murdered. I'm going back to the police. One way or another, we have to find out who's behind all this."

The girls buzzed, united as bees bringing fresh honey back to the hive—and Eastwick was *their* hive, so there was no question about their wanting to protect it. Any other time, Emma would have been roiled up as the rest of them, and she was relieved to hear that the reason for Caroline's suicide attempt had finally come out in the open. Still, Garrett's uncovering his sister's secret stirred her own heart-sick situation again. It was so like him to get that secret out of Caro no matter what it took. Garrett would go to the ends of the earth for those he loved. But knowing that only gave Emma a fresh taste of despair…until she suddenly realized that all conversation at the table had stopped.

That never happened. Not with the Debs. Even when there wasn't a crisis of events, they talked each others' ears off. So the sudden silence made Emma's head shoot up. "What…?" she began to ask.

But then she saw the man wending his way from the doorway to their table. It was hard to guess why or how Garrett snared the women's complete attention, but Emma wasted no time wondering about that.

He searched the crowd, searched all the faces—found hers.

Their eyes met.

He kept coming. His every footstep brought a new race to her heart. He never faltered, never looked away, never glanced at the other women. When he reached the table, he just reached out a hand and snagged her wrist.

"I'm sorry to interrupt your lunch, ladies, but I need Emma. Right now," he said. "And this won't wait."

Twelve

Emma had no logical reason to feel her heart suddenly rush with hope. But it did. Just from seeing him. Just from feeling his hand clasped in hers. She didn't know why he'd sought her out, didn't care. For those few moments, just being with him seemed enough to stave off that awful despair chewing on her heart.

But when he ushered her into the passenger seat of his car, she couldn't help asking, "Where are we going?"

"A place where we can talk with no interruptions, guaranteed. All right?"

"Yes." It was more than all right. He wanted to talk to her—but she so fiercely wanted to talk to him.

She watched him, not the road, as he drove. For four days and four nights she'd pined for him. She'd hurt so badly to think he'd believe she was a gold digger.

But those same four days and four nights she'd done enough analyzing and agonizing to face some scary truths. The Debs' lunch today had reechoed one of her discoveries. Garrett had discovered his sister's secret, dug and dug and dug until he'd found a way to help Caroline—then gone after helping her whole hog. That was how he lived, who he was.

Emma had so fallen for the right man—a man who'd climb K2 and back for someone he loved.

She just hadn't realized how his character directly applied to how he'd reacted to her days before.

"I've thought over a lot of things over the past few days," he said quietly.

"So have I." When he didn't add anything more personal, she tried taking a different conversational track. "Caroline had a lot to say at lunch today. It sounds as if everything's going to work out all right for her. Thanks to you."

"There's no happy ending in the bank yet. Nothing can be completely resolved until the blackmailer is caught. But…"

"But what?"

"But I've done all I can do. The rest is up to her husband. And the police." Garrett shot her a quick glance. "I love my sister, but I have other things on my mind right now."

That sounded ominous. When she'd thought about seeing him again, Emma had assumed she'd rush to say all the things she wanted and needed to. Yet the fear of his rejecting her, of losing him a second time, kept a thick knot in her throat. She couldn't tell from his expression what he wanted to say or what he wanted.

They passed the town, the wealthy suburbs, hit the coast road. Less than five minutes later he turned in at a private airstrip. A silver Lear sat on the runway, stairs pulled up to the open door. A dark haired man stood in the doorway. Garrett drove the car right on the tarmac to the steps.

"What on earth—?"

"Just a private place to talk," he assured her.

That was a lie. She could see it in his eyes. But the plane and location were so mystifying that she decided to just wait him out, see what he was up to.

Garrett climbed out of the car and spoke to the man who descended from the plane—Emma thought she heard the guy was called Doug. Then Garrett came back for her.

"This is my driver from New York, Emma. I have to trade this set of wheels for another."

It seemed even more mystifying that he'd be fussing with car or business problems at this precise moment, but she went along. The minute she stepped out, Doug immediately climbed in and took off with the car. Which was fine. Only there wasn't another vehicle in sight.

Garrett motioned her toward the plane. "I know it looks crazy. But it's the one place in the universe where I can guarantee that no one, absolutely no one, will either interrupt or find us."

She never saw nerves in his expression, his posture, yet something about him was so completely different that it finally registered: he was scared. Damn near too scared to breathe. At least, to breathe normally.

She climbed the steps ahead of him and ducked inside. She'd been in private planes all her life, but not this specific Lear. The inside had been customized to resemble a living room. The couches and easy chairs had seat belts, but otherwise, the white leather furnishings and polished cherry could have been in any comfortable den.

Once they were inside, out of the bright sunlight, and she was finally completely alone with him, she whirled around. It was all she could take of mystifying mysteries and waiting.

"I was wrong, Garrett," she whispered.

"No. Not you. I was the one who was wrong."

She shook her head. "You assumed that money mattered to me. I wanted to deny that from here to Poughkeepsie. But when I looked at my life, really looked, I realized you had every reason to make that assumption." She gulped, then spilled more out. "I've had everything I ever wanted. Just took it for granted. I've been spoiled."

"No, you haven't, Em. Everywhere I look, you're giving something to others—"

"And I love giving. But it's been easy for me, Garrett. Easy for me to keep taking handouts from my parents because I always had the excuse of the trust fund coming in. But the reality was that it was easy to spend, easy to live exactly how I wanted to live. I guess it should have been obvious to me, but a woman almost thirty who's never lived within her means is darn spoiled. From your viewpoint, I'd be amazed if you hadn't seen me as selfish."

Finally that calm, quiet expression in his face seemed to crack. Suddenly his dark eyes looked liquid and naked, raw with vulnerability and something else. "Emma, you are positively the least selfish person I know."

"Garrett, I'm trying to say that I understand. Why you thought I might have…pursued…you, knowing there was a threat to my inheritance. I realize now that you had every reason to think of me as materialistic—"

"Stop." He scrabbled a hand through his hair. "I admit

it, Emma. I did think that—for a short period of time. Where you saw that judgment as an insult, I just thought of it as life. The practical way people are in real life. But then I did some soul-searching, too. And realized that growing up, all the values I saw stemmed from money. No one in my family made a choice that didn't include money. Value—all value—was defined by money."

"I understand."

"No. You can't. It was a knee-jerk reaction for me to respond that way. I didn't want you to need me only because of money. I didn't want you to believe I gave a damn about your money, either. I just wanted there to be an *us*. So I just said the first thing that would make that money problem disappear."

Emma jolted in shock when a stranger showed up in the cockpit door. She hadn't realized anyone else was on the plane. The gray-haired man raised a hand in greeting, then said quickly, "We've been cleared for takeoff, Mr. Keating. Five minutes." He turned, pulled the plane's door shut then disappeared back into the cockpit after sealing that door closed, too.

Emma shot startled eyes at Garrett.

"Aw, hell," he said. "If I were a knight in shining armor, I could pull this off the way it should be. But I'm not, Em. This is the thing—I can have you back before work tomorrow if you need to be, but there's somewhere I want you to fly with me now. Just say yes."

For that expression in his eyes, she'd have said yes to anything he asked. He strapped her in next to him just in time to hear the engines start up. Before they zoomed into the air, though, he put two boxes in her lap. They were both sapphire velvet—one a small square box and the other a large oblong shape.

The jet had leveled off above the clouds before he let her open the big one. She found all kinds of papers—a lab report on blood tests, the deed and title to Color, the deed to a brownstone in Manhattan, a marriage license, an appointment with an unknown man for later that same day.

She looked up, both overwhelmed and confused.

"The appointment is with an artist. The second box is empty, Emma, for now, because I didn't want an heirloom or a standard ring. I wanted a design created that's uniquely for you and only you. And I thought it'd be a good time to do that right after dinner."

"After dinner," she said faintly.

"Yeah. I thought we could get married first. I had to call your doctor to get the blood-test form. And I bought a couple of plain gold matching bands so we could have a token before your real ring is ready."

"Married," she said faintly.

"I was thinking about buying you an island. Just a small one. For a getaway. A place where we could skinny-dip in the pale blue water and sleep on a bed of rose petals and watch sunrises and sunsets together. But I haven't had a chance yet to—"

"A chance," she said faintly.

He unhooked her safety belt, then his, then, as if she weighed less than a cotton puff, pulled her directly on his lap. "Emma, please don't argue with me. We need to be married before your thirtieth birthday. I don't want you ever, ever worried about your independence. That's why I put all these papers in motion, including a trust for you—

a trust that's all yours. No matter what happens to me. And as far as *your* trust, cookie—"

He motioned when she tried to speak.

"As far as your trust, I think we could save that for our kids. Then you can put it completely out of your mind, never think about it again. But the rest of the plan, we could keep it between us."

"Between us," she echoed one last time.

"You could divorce me after your birthday if you want. But this solves everything, you know? You don't have to fret inheritances or anything else, but you can still get what should have been yours from the start. And while we're together, I'd have the chance to woo you, cookie. To experiment with being a better white knight. To love you the way I want you to be loved—"

It took a kiss to shut him up. Who'd have guessed her so controlled, so strong Garrett could be so vulnerable? Yet when her lips grazed his, her lover came to life. A soft kiss became richer, sweeter, deeper. Eyes closed, she offered him her heart, winding her arms around him, sealing him close to her.

Finally she lifted her head and frowned. "Did I mention that I was crazy about you?"

"I don't think it came up," he said.

"Did I mention how much I love you?"

"No. But I was starting to believe it."

"Only starting?" She zoomed down again and forced him to suffer through another set of kisses, a scale of kisses and touches and embraces that threatened to crumble his control…and for darn sure, hers.

"I believe, I believe," he whispered tenderly.

"I like that phrase you used about our building something only between us," she whispered back. "We can do it, Garrett. Build our own dynasty, our own way. Build a house. Build a family."

"Build a life. With love framing every day in it," he said. And that was the last either of them wasted time talking.

* * * * *

Look for the next book in the
SECRET LIVES OF SOCIETY WIVES *miniseries!*
THE ONE-WEEK WIFE by Patricia Kay
coming from Silhouette Desire July 2006.

Page-turning drama…

Exotic, glamorous locations…

Intense emotion and passionate seduction…

Sheikhs, princes and billionaire tycoons…

This summer, may we suggest:

THE SHEIKH'S DISOBEDIENT BRIDE
by Jane Porter

On sale June.

AT THE GREEK TYCOON'S BIDDING
by Cathy Williams

On sale July.

THE ITALIAN MILLIONAIRE'S VIRGIN WIFE

On sale August.

With new titles to choose from every month, discover a world of romance in our books written by internationally bestselling authors.

Silhouette®
Desire

COMING NEXT MONTH

#1735 UNDER DEEPEST COVER—Kara Lennox
The Elliotts
He needed her help, she needed his protection, but posing as
lovers could prove to be risky…and every bit the scandal.

#1736 THE TEXAN'S CONVENIENT MARRIAGE—
Peggy Moreland
A Piece of Texas
A Texan's plans to keep his merger of convenience casual are
ruined when passion enters the marriage bed.

#1737 THE ONE-WEEK WIFE—Patricia Kay
Secret Lives of Society Wives
A fake honeymoon turns into an ardent escapade when the
wedding planner plays the millionaire's wife for a week.

#1738 EXPOSING THE EXECUTIVE'S SECRETS—
Emilie Rose
Trust Fund Affairs
Buying her ex at a charity bachelor auction seemed the perfect
way to settle the score, until the sparks start flying again.

#1739 THE MILLIONAIRE'S PREGNANT MISTRESS—
Michelle Celmer
Rich and Reclusive
A stolen night of passion. An unplanned pregnancy. Was a forced
marriage next?

#1740 TO CLAIM HIS OWN—Mary Lynn Baxter
He'd returned to claim his child—but his son's beautiful guardian
was not giving up without a fight.